SYLVIE GINESTET

THE RECOUVRANCE

The Imhumvamps: Volume 2

Previously published

The Quest – The Imhumvamps V1   February 2014
Shadow Play   September 2015

In french

Le Miracle, Les Imhumvamps T1   September 2012
La Recouvrance, Les Imhumvamps T2   September 2014
Les ombres s'amusent   February 2015
Une vie pour la vie, Les Imhumvamps T3   October 2015
Le Livre des âmes, Bethany T1   February 2016

ISBN: 978-2-930895-01-7
Formal deposit: D/2016/Ginestet Sylvie, Publisher

First published in French under the title *"La Recouvrance"* in 2014. Translated from French by *"Intuitive Translations"*, Torquay, United Kingdom.

SYLVIE GINESTET

THE RECOUVRANCE

The Imhumvamps: Volume 2

Thanks you, Graham for your precious help.

1. The Train

The train isn't my preferred means of transport, especially since my transformation. I like to be free to move around.

This Monday, I had to go to a meeting in the south of France, far away from home and far away from everything. Since my return among the humans, this was the second time I found myself locked in a high-speed train for a few hours, but I still preferred it to flying. The meeting would begin very early in the morning, so I opted to travel on Sunday evening. The journey would take three hours, but we were already leaving twenty-five minutes late. It seemed that the train was waiting for latecomers for once.

Despite the lateness of the hour, our carriage was almost full. Most people were there because they were going on holiday; in this case, Easter. Spring was mild this year, an incentive for a change of scene. A foretaste maybe of a hot and dry summer. My first as a vampire.

The train finally sped off and the journey could at last begin. Everyone settled themselves down, some brought out laptops, others those new touch-screen tablets which were all the rage.

One row ahead of me on the right, a man dressed in black, who certainly wasn't heading off on holiday, was playing on his mobile phone; often pushing his glasses up along his nose, displaying quite some anxiety. Regularly, people were passing along the aisle to get to the dining-car or to stretch their legs. And this was only the start of the journey.

Beside me sat a young man, simply dressed in jeans, trainers and a t-shirt. After enjoying some cold pizza which he brought out from a Tupperware box, he sat at his laptop. The train didn't seem to be going as fast as it should; a conductor's announcement confirmed my thoughts. I wondered how late we would be in the end. Our journey had started badly.

Always worried about me, Darren didn't like me to be out of my comfort zone, even if after four months among humans, no untoward incident had occurred. When, like tonight, I would have to be enclosed somewhere with them, I'd take refuge in my musical world. As long as nothing from outside caught my attention, all would be well. What reassured me the most was the fact that Darren could follow my tracks thanks to my mobile phone, equipped with a GPS system connected to his. This small security measure reassured us a little. I had to pay particular attention to feeding myself at fixed times, and to avoid emergency situations, especially when travelling, because I wasn't a predator. I was a therapeutic vampire; unique, as I liked to say. Certainly an abomination in the eyes of some, but that didn't matter.

I thought of Darren; I was missing him. We were in touch as often as we could be, which was to say not a lot.

He was very much occupied with his business, and me with my work and my life as a human. Admittedly we exchanged many emails and text messages, but his absence made me feel terribly devastated. Four months was too long!

Further along the compartment, a man sat sweating nervously; his behaviour was suspicious. This kind of detail caught my attention!

The train continued on more and more slowly, the journey seemingly endless. I was still watching him; he was mopping his forehead, putting his handkerchief awkwardly into his pocket. He was looking all around, and above all at his watch, every two minutes. I decided to do something that I would never normally do: I forbade myself from doing it with humans, although in some meetings it was very funny. I was going to attempt to probe his mind, since his anxiety was making me nervous; as this was neither the time nor the place for nervousness. I needed to concentrate, so I turned off the sound of my music player whilst keeping the headphones on. This way I wouldn't receive any interference from the other humans present nearby.

But I couldn't manage to get into his head. Alongside him there was a seat free; I picked up my things and went to sit over there in the hope that the proximity would help.

"Is this seat free?" I asked politely. "I don't feel good to be working while I'm sitting back-to-front, it makes me nauseous. May I?"

"Do whatever you like," replied the man.

I sat in silence, concentrating on him. My instinct hadn't misled me. I focused on him, taking care not to be spotted, but he was so preoccupied that he didn't notice. I picked out snippets of thoughts, and the little I did hear was very disconcerting: "I must calm down"... "They said everything would be fine"... "I'm only here to create a diversion"... "I've nothing to be afraid of"... "Why has this girl come to sit here?"... With this thought, I averted my gaze slightly towards the window... "She's pretty"... "I have to stay focused on my task"... "Stay calm"...

I decided to send a message to Darren, telling him what I had overheard in the head of a passenger; I figured he was up to something, without doubt nothing good. The train had finally reached its normal speed, the man still had confused thoughts, and I still didn't understand what was going on here. We were approaching Dijon, it being already dark outside when, suddenly, he stood up brandishing a weapon.

"You will listen to me; obey me and everything will be fine. We will arrive at Dijon in a few minutes. You;" he pointed to a blonde woman carrying a young child, "you will get off with your squealing rabble and you will give this letter to the station manager, right into his hands."

"Okay," she hurriedly said.

She would have accepted anything from the moment she realised she would come out safe and sound. Already up, she took the letter and walked hastily to the exit doors, holding her children close to her.

"Very good, young lady, I like obedience. Perfect," he said, following them with one eye.

Then, he pointed to a good proportion of the passengers, and ordered them to prepare to disembark. I watched, hoping that he was also referring to me and would let me leave.

"You," he said, pointing with his weapon, "you wanted to come and sit here so you'll stay."

Next, he handed a bag to a man; asking him to go around among the remainder of us in order to confiscate our mobile phones, PCs and my handbag; which immediately made me feel uneasy because it contained my capsules. He gathered everything up and put it all in a large travel bag, and then separated us around the seats. I counted eight hostages apart from myself.

Then he headed over to the group who were about to get off.

"Except for you," he began, staring at the woman, "nobody tell anyone about what's happening here, I've got my eye on you, and my associates will be on the dock. So be warned!" he shouted, brandishing his weapon again.

Nobody answered, all nodding in silent agreement, too happy just to be getting out of there. The woman fixed me with a sorry look, a little guilty at faring better than me; she held her children tightly to her, to make me understand that she couldn't do any differently, to which I smiled in response. The TGV came to a halt, we watched the people go off to their freedom; and three minutes later, which seemed like an eternity, the train continued on its way.

We were silent, the hostage-taker as well. I was thinking about how I would get my possessions back, and was really hoping Darren had received my message. Seeing that I'd remained silent following any reply, he would understand that I was in danger, and perhaps he would come to find me.

Suddenly, a strange clanking could be heard originating from the rear of the train and I could see through the glass interconnecting doors of our carriage, that the carriages behind us had become separated and were gradually getting further and further away. Someone had uncoupled a section of the train; us, we continued to move onwards; he had told the truth, he couldn't have done it alone!

It was only half an hour later when a second clanking occurred. After ten more minutes, what was left of our means of transport came to a stop in the middle of nowhere. We were surrounded by darkness. The man's silence did nothing to reassure me.

"Why are you doing this?" I asked.

"The less you know, the better," he replied, peering outside.

He was waiting for someone or something. I started becoming ice-cold, which wasn't normal at all. I wasn't supposed to have felt such a coldness as this, which overcame me, making me shiver. I felt feverish, as if I had a temperature, and this was no time to be ill. Deprived of my purse, it came into my mind that I had unintentionally skipped a meal, so to speak. I'd just run out of time and now I was paying the price for it.

One more hour passed without the slightest movement, either outside or inside. The man turned around, wondering aloud what his accomplices were doing, and why they were so slow to respond. I had no idea of the purpose of this operation; hunger began to take hold and my mind was focusing more on my emptiness than on that stupid guy who had decided to spoil our lives.

Suddenly the TGV lights went out, creating a slight panic among my companions in misfortune. The hostage-taker stood up in the dark, warning us to be quiet. I sensed that he was on the verge of a nervous breakdown; things weren't going at all as he had expected, everything had become complicated and hence it would be really dangerous. Personally, I had nothing to fear, but for the others it was different. I could feel myself becoming more and more hungry; inwardly I thanked the Gods for this present interruption, because my lack of food was starting to be physically noticeable. These people were panicked enough already, without needing to add a vampire to their list of worries.

My acuity in the dark did me a great service, it permitted me to see someone approaching us. I didn't dare intervene, supposing that this would help the hostage-taker, but I feared what was about to follow and my intuition gave me good reason.

I saw his fist landing on the nose of our enemy who screamed in surprise and pain, a trickle of blood flowed from his nose, which he wiped with the back of his sleeve. He dropped his weapon, which I instinctively pushed under the seat with my foot. He swore. The other man tried to grab him, which wasn't so easy because of the little tables between them. A strange silence descended within the train; people could hear the blows of a fight without knowing who was winning.

The perpetrator stooped down to pick up his weapon, groping in the dark, which made our saviour lose his balance. Suddenly he reappeared from beneath the seat, gun in hand, to strike a nasty blow to the head, with which all our hopes of rescue evaporated, as the body of our hero fell heavily to the ground.

The leader regained his composure.

"The next person to try that, I'll kill him," he shouted.

This made the silence in the car become even heavier.

The smell of blood came to me, slyly, slowly, it filled my nostrils and stimulated my new instincts. The situation was becoming critical. In my head a stack of ideas were jostling around. So easily, I could either satisfy my thirst by jumping on this man, and thus liberate everyone from this madman; or wait for someone to free us, knowing neither where nor how, nor specifically when. I was hoping that Darren had read the message I'd sent before that chap confiscated our belongings.

The blood, so near, brought about the beginning of a transformation which I was trying so very hard to contain.

"Will you allow me to go to the bathroom?" I asked the man, thinking on the hoof.

"Silence!" he cried.

I put one of my hands on his arm trying to calm him down.

"Please," I said softly.

He thought for a moment before answering.

"No dirty tricks, okay... I'll wait for you here in five minutes," he said, finally.

His assent aroused other voices in the carriage, demanding the same thing, which made sense considering the length of time that we'd been glued to our seats. The desire to relieve oneself or simply to stretch one's legs had become pressing. Except that me, I just wanted to hide, to calm myself down in order to regain a normal appearance.

"Okay... Okay, let's calm down; you first," he said, pushing me. "The rest of you," he paused for a time, "wait until she returns."

I was heading towards the toilet when the lights came back on. A wave of fear ran through me, I turned back around towards the carriage and saw a look from a man who was staring at me, horrified, apparently because he'd seen. Ignoring him, I quickly continued on my way. Passing my tongue over my teeth confirmed what I feared. I was, in those few moments, no longer myself, however I might say it.

I closed the door behind me and took a breath. The room was cramped and smelled of urine which had the effect of calming me down a bit. I approached the mirror and understood why he'd been frightened. My skin was white, sickly; my eyes were ringed with black, my pupils almost white. I opened my mouth, my elongated canines confirmed to me that I could indeed be frightening. This was the first time that I'd found myself so hungry and thirsty, such that I didn't know whether I could recover my human appearance after only recuperating for five minutes. The time allotted to me was too short for anything other than to relieve myself. I tried it without succeeding. So I chose another option; although I couldn't become human, perhaps I could camouflage myself a little. Rummaging through the pockets of my jacket, I took out my sunglasses and found some foundation, a gimmick that I hadn't used for quite some while. I did myself some make-up; it would be enough just to keep my mouth shut and this scheme would suffice for the moment.

In the distance, I heard our bandit shouting "go and see what she's doing," addressing himself to someone. A few seconds later, somebody knocked on the bathroom door.

"Are you okay miss?" Asked a male voice.

I slowly opened the door, smiling discreetly to the man. My look, from behind my glasses, gave me an advantage.

"Yes thank you," I said, hurrying back to my place.

Showing his anxiety, he grabbed me by the arm, stopping me dead.

"You're sick, I'm a doctor; I can help you," he insisted.

"No, I don't think so," I told him. "I already have a doctor, thanks."

"Let me quickly examine you, before this madman comes along," he said, attempting to put his hand on my forehead.

"Don't touch me!" I almost cried out, before removing his hand from my arm.

The icy touch of my palm made him recoil. I freed myself from his grip and got back to my place.

"I'm very well; leave me in peace."

I sat back down, trying to keep calm, perturbed by what this man wanted with me. Was he really a doctor, or was he one of those vampire-hunters? I felt too exhausted to try responding to my interrogation. I needed to stay on my guard and think about Darren; his advice, his considerations. But would I see evil from now on in every human? Emerging from my thoughts, my eyes again rested on him when he returned to his seat. I was too weak to probe his mind and that of our aggressor, I needed to nourish myself.

"You took your time!" Said the hostage-taker.

"I don't feel very well, I'm sorry. Trains always make me sick, it's simply travel-sickness."

I emphasised that final phrase, staring through my glasses at the alleged doctor. He persisted in staring at me, whilst writing things in a notebook. This last detail unsettled me. For me, there was much more than one danger aboard the carriage.

At this instant, a dull thud resonated around us, coming from the roof above our heads. The hostage-taker got up and ran through the carriage looking through each window to look for any activity, but nothing could be seen outside. The man asked some of us whether we had heard something; all answered, with fearful voices, in the affirmative.

A second then a third impact was audible; we all had our eyes glued to the ceiling. Glimmers of hope began to spread across the faces of my fellow travellers. The man meanwhile was sweating profusely. It was quite apparently not the police, unless an elite team had managed to get themselves close to this train, immobilised in the middle of nowhere. I don't know why but I had my doubts.

Nothing further happened during the thirty minutes that followed, which made us think that maybe it had just been some animals. The police wouldn't leave us like this, they would at least try to communicate with the man, who seemed not to be coping very well. I felt more and more feeble and therefore vulnerable! My nails had become all black. Then I heard a very distant voice.

"Lilly, answer me... How it's going? Where are you situated?"

I opened my eyes; Darren's voice resounded in my head.

"Darren?"

"How are you feeling?"

I felt a relief coming through his voice.

"Not very well I must admit, he confiscated our bags and our phones. I'm very weak. I'm sitting next to him, he's bleeding. I'm sorry I can't control the changes in my body. I'm so sorry Darren."

"Don't worry for now. We're coming in; protect yourself."

I barely had time to get myself down, before an enormous explosion of broken glass rang out, intermingled with screams of panic.

I recognised Hector's voice, which exclaimed *"Police, everybody on the floor."* They threw smoke-bombs all around us. The hostage-taker didn't even have time to react and grab his weapon; someone had already pulled him unceremoniously out through the window of the carriage. I heard the dry crack of a neck being broken. Immediately afterwards, Darren lifted me out and took me off the train, hidden from view. With my eyes closed, I nourished myself first of all on his scent. He put me on the ground, still keeping me in his arms. He tilted his head toward me, offering me his neck.

"Feed yourself my Lilly," he softly invited me, stroking my hair.

"Not like that, I don't want to."

I put my hand on his cheek, I was so exhausted.

"You have to, your situation is now too far advanced to satisfy your needs with just our capsules. Bite me now," he ordered me.

"I don't have the strength, I'm sorry," I replied, resting my head on his shoulder.

He tore a gash in his wrist with a cut from a sharp tooth; the blood began to flow immediately. He brought it up to my mouth, he had no need to tell me again to drink. The smell attracted me to it straight away. I took his arm and bit into his already open flesh.

One thing I'd never told him about was the pleasure I felt when my canines penetrated his skin, when the blood invaded my mouth to spread itself throughout my body, giving me an indescribable sense of well-being. The capsules didn't give me such a feeling. What should I conclude? I wasn't a predator but I did have those instincts; I shouldn't feel that way. Once I'd had enough, Darren gently removed his wrist, which he wiped clean; I passed my hand over my mouth to remove the still-visible blood. He handed me two capsules which I swallowed straight away without water; I felt much better, almost normal. I looked at his wrist, it was already better, healed.

"There was a man in the carriage," I began to say.

"He's dead, Lilly..."

"Not that one; another," I interrupted.

"How do you mean, which other man?" He asked, looking worried.

"He saw me, let's say, in a state of weakness. He told me he was a doctor and touched me. Even though I told him to leave me in peace, just touching my skin made him recoil. Then, he went to sit back down and I saw him taking notes."

"Come, show him to me," he said, walking towards the door of the carriage.

I followed him silently, wondering what was going to happen; I'd had my share of surprises today. At the door, they had all regrouped and were talking; I smiled to Hector and Vic.

Hector gave me a nod and handed me my bag.

"I suppose this is yours, Miss."

"Oh! Thank you Sir, it is indeed mine."

I quickly looked inside the bag and could see that nothing was missing. Next, I looked for the other man, the doctor. He was next to the lifeless body of the hostage-taker on the other side of the carriage.

"It's that man over there who's crouching beside the corpse," I pointed out to Darren.

"Stay here, I'll go and look," he told me, starting to walk.

It was at that precise moment, and only just then, when I realised that Darren, Hector and Vic were dressed in police uniforms. They had made every effort to be credible in the eyes of the humans.

My attention turned back to Darren, I heard him speak.

"Good evening Sir, are you all right?" Darren asked the doctor, bending down near the two men.

"I'm okay, but he's dead," he replied, pointing to the body.

"It's a risk that he surely knew about. Did he mention anything about this hostage-taking?"

"Nothing at all, sorry. Why did you remove the woman to the outside?" He asked, getting up.

"We thought that she might be his accomplice, they were sitting next to each other," said Darren, naturally.

"Ah! But not so at all, believe me. She seemed to be ill. How is she now?" He asked again, turning his head towards me.

"She's better, I gave her a health-bar, it's not very good but it peps a person up a bit," said Darren, smiling.

"And that was enough?"

"I think so, yes, she's on her feet. Why so much interest in her? Do you have a problem with something?"

"I'm concerned about her health. I am a doctor, you understand."

He showed his business card to Darren, while continuing to talk.

"I still don't know about her. I found her very pale and very cold; her skin I mean."

"Oh I see, I didn't notice any such thing."

Darren beckoned me over.

"Come here please, Miss."

"Yes?" I headed over towards them.

"This gentleman," Darren said, pointing him out to me, "who is a doctor, told me that you are ill. Are you all right, Miss?"

I pretended to be surprised.

"Yes, I'm fine. I had a moment of weakness before all the action but now I'm better thanks to that abominable cereal bar," I finished speaking, watching Darren.

"You see, she's fine. Now we're reassured."

The man made a movement in my direction; I instinctively recoiled.

"What do you want with me? I'm feeling all right, okay!"

I was beginning to lose patience. Looking at Darren I said aloud:

"You see, I told you..."

In my head, I heard his answer.

"Lilly! Don't say that, he doesn't know we've already spoken about him!"

Now, the man was looking at us in turn, passing from Darren over to me, staring at us.

"You know each other?" He asked, a hint of worry in his voice.

"No," we answered, in unison.

"One moment please Sir," instructed Darren, laying his hand on the shoulder of the man, who grimaced.

I had placed us in a difficult situation.

I saw Vic leading the ex-hostages into a car. I turned quickly to Darren.

"Where's he taking them, please?"

"To the police station," he replied, still holding on to the doctor.

I looked at the man, who seemed to be suffering; his fate was worrying me now. Hector came over to join us. There were now only four of us here. Darren released his grip on the man.

"My colleague will take care of you, Sir," he said, gently pushing him towards Hector.

The man fixed me in his gaze; how much did he understand? His look was charged with questions. What could I tell him? That his curiosity had probably got him killed? I didn't sense any danger coming from him, I closed my eyes and tried to listen, he had to be thinking! Actually he was doing so: "These guys are not cops... and not that madman's other accomplices, otherwise he would still be alive... They had come for this girl, and only for her..." Strangely, we were staring at each other: I had the impression that he knew I was there, inside his head... "You can hear me can't you?" Then he said not a word more, at least he tried to fall silent. Then he carried on: "It's apparent from your look. What are you exactly, aliens? Genetically engineered people? ... Are you going to kill me? ..."

"Answer me Miss," he finished by saying.

"Answer to what? You haven't asked anything."

"Are you sure?" He insisted.

I didn't respond with anything, but questioned Darren.

"Can he sense me inside his head? Perceive that I'm listening to him?"

"Not that I know of, he's just suspecting it."

"But how?"

"What's emanating from you, your simple kindness, remains so human.

I stood there thinking, this man was different.

"Give him the choice, please."

"No Lilly, my family no longer do that!"

I went over to Darren, it was good to see him; I'd missed him so much. I fixed him in my gaze.

"You don't commit murder. You don't kill for the sake of killing, but can't you change those who deserve to be, rather than kill them for safety's sake?" I argued.

"In what way does he merit this?"

The situation must have seemed strange, seen from the outside.

"I don't know, an intuition. He's scared and doesn't know what we are. And I know that if you asked Vic to leave with the others and Hector to come back with us, it's because you don't want to leave any trace. Am I mistaken, Darren?"

"No, you're not mistaken. Are those your only arguments for saving this man?

"Give him the choice. He is a doctor and he can be useful to us, to the family I mean."

Hector grabbed the man by the arm and began to drag him away; now he was really scared. I felt it, I heard him asking me for help.

"One moment Hector please," I said loudly.

"Hector?" Said the man, staring at me.

The situation was getting worse, I turned towards Darren.

"You can save him, he did nothing wrong! He wanted to help me in some way."

"Are you going to ask me this each time you come in contact with a human who is a bit different?"

"No, I can't actually promise you that this will be the last time, but please."

"What's happening?" The man asked; the silence would have been stressing him a little more.

"Shut up!" I caught myself saying, which immediately quietened him down.

"Sir?" Asked Hector.

Darren approached the man, who took a step back. His demand surprised me:

"Give me your papers."

The man obeyed without hesitation, handing his wallet to Darren, who put it in his pocket without even opening it.

"Well, Sir, you've maybe just been saved by this girl; you have her to thank for this respite. Let's go, Hector," Darren announced.

Hector again grabbed the man and forced him to head towards the car. I could hear police sirens in the distance; it was time to leave. Darren stopped me in my tracks, I was scared momentarily.

"My little Lilly," he ran his hand tenderly over my cheek, "you would save the whole world if you could. We can't, you know."

"Yes I know, but he doesn't deserve to die. I feel it, Darren. So it'll be his choice whether he wants to stay alive and join us."

"Do you remember the misery you underwent to become one of us?"

"Yes, how could I forget those moments?"

He took my hand then we caught up with Hector, and our survivor already seated in the back. Darren took the wheel; I sat next to him. The man had turned pale and I understood why. No words were spoken during our trip, which went on for quite some time. Right from the open countryside near Dijon all the way to the castle, it was rather a long trek. I carefully looked in my mirror and realised that the man was asleep; so many emotions for one single night for this human. This went for me too, but, for the time being, I had saved him. Darren didn't seem angry, and as for Hector; he followed the beck and call of his master's decisions, so…

I turned towards him,

"You knocked him out?"

"No, he's just asleep, but I had considered it in case he asked too many questions or showed any resistance."

"Hmm! I see," I said, turning back to face the road.

I noticed that Darren was smiling.

"Anyway, I'm glad to see you, I would've preferred it in different circumstances, of course."

Arriving at the chateau, I saw Martin's car in the courtyard, and the living room lights were on. We got out of our vehicle, and Darren asked me to go to bed; I obeyed in silence. As for them, they took the man and headed over to the right-hand side of the chateau. I cast a final glance at him and at the group; he was terrified. The door closed behind them; I no longer had any influence.

After this incident, Darren didn't want me to return to work any longer, it was too dangerous from his point of view; there were too many situations where I could lose my composure. It's true that, if I hadn't controlled myself, our aggressor could have been dead a few hours sooner. Of course, the result would have been the same for him, but not for me. I'd mastered my thirst and had good reflexes.

The danger had been very real. Why are humans always so eager for malice or violence? More and more, I told myself that the human race only served to put itself in peril. The proof was the very few seconds it took to overcome this madman, and the fact that facing a vampire, a human was not as powerful, surprisingly or not.

I'd again put the family in danger with my actions; my obstinate determination to act like a human, despite having non-human needs. What I'd seen was, that even if Darren's family were peaceful, this changed completely when one of their own was in danger. I remained convinced that if it had been anyone else they would have done the same. Their loyalty was a strength.

It wasn't too hard for Darren to convince me, he asked Martin to arrange me a long-term break from work, blaming a workplace accident, such that I wouldn't lose any money. Martin had become my new regular family doctor, it was much easier this way. No more need to justify myself. As for Professor Moonroe; the latest news was that he was still committed in an institution.

In the eyes of the humans, I was still alive but weakened, and in need of taking a rest after the incident on the train.

The investigation regarding the hijacking was ongoing. The front of the train had continued its journey without any hindrance; in the rear carriages, which had been detached, there had been only luggage.

We still don't know why the hostage-taker had done this. Nothing in the individual's home had enabled anyone to determine the reasons for his actions, and his accomplices remained untraceable. Regarding his sudden death, the police had concluded that this had been as a result of a settling of scores, seeing as his was the only body found at the scene.

This minor incident would remain a mystery.

2. The Departure

Early in the morning, Darren burst into my room.

"We're going away, Lilly!"

I turned to him, surprised by two things; the first being that he'd entered into my room without knocking, and the second being what he'd said.

"Where to?"

He approached me slowly, his eyes expressing excitement; whatever the thing that he was about to say, it would be difficult to resist.

"To Ireland!"

Darren had decided that the time had come to return to our roots, for me as much as for him. He took my hands in his.

"You don't feel like it?"

"I don't know," I replied softly.

"But don't you want to know who your father is? Don't you want to know your history?"

"Yes, of course, but is this a good time for it?"

"There's neither a good time nor a bad time. There is just one moment, and it's now. We could, equally, pay a visit to Marie. You should get out of here and take your mind off things. Also I'd like to show you my country."

"Maybe, but I have to go back home and tell Sandrine that I'll be away again. And my cats?"

"We'll go together, Sandrine should understand very well that after such an event as you've just endured, you'll need space to breathe again. As for your cats, we'll bring them back here; we'll also be able to close up your house and allow you to become less indebted in that respect. What do you think?" he finally asked me.

"I see you've already planned everything, I can only bow down before such organisation, and above all, such gusto."

"A very wise decision," he said, leaving the room.

Then I heard him shouting from the end of the hallway.

"I'm going to prepare the helicopter; meet you down there in fifteen minutes."

Slowly, I let my arms drop beside me. Fifteen minutes to prepare my luggage: Darren was a man indeed, without any doubt. I'd opened up my bag just a few hours ago and I'd put everything I had in it, which is to say; little. I was only intending to have left the house for two days of meetings and now, I was leaving for Ireland.

Darren had already planned everything, our flight was scheduled during the following two hours! This neither give us time to go home and get my things and my cats, nor the opportunity to inform Sandrine.

So I grabbed the phone, to warn her about my latest absence, and also to say that someone would come to collect the cats; and therefore that if she could just keep them locked in the house it would make things easier. She posed very few questions, because during the few months we had been close again, apparently I spent my time talking about Darren and the moments I shared with him; so on the announcement of my departure, she didn't object, and advised me to seize this opportunity; which made me smile.

Fifteen minutes later, I was finally ready at the foot of the stairs waiting for Darren. He arrived a few minutes later. Looking at my bag apologetically, he said:

"We'll buy whatever you need when we get there."

He took the bag and my hand, then gallantly opened the door for me.

Darren was so overjoyed, it was almost indecent. He took his seat, and turned his head towards me; he looked very happy. He pulled away at high speed.

"Can I ask you a question?" I asked.

"Yes of course."

"Where is the doctor from the train?"

I needed to know. He glanced briefly at me, concentrating on the road.

"We gave him the choice."

"And what did he choose?"

"He hasn't yet decided, so we've given him more time."

"You're telling me that you told him everything about us, and that you've allowed him time to make a decision: That's irresponsible, Darren!"

"You were right about one thing, this human is trustworthy. Martin read his mind. He felt no danger there, unless this man is very clever; but I strongly doubt whether he could fool Martin."

"And where is he now? I didn't see him at the chateau," I asked, surprised by their decision.

"Vic's looking after him, he's keeping him at the club. We should still be cautious. Don't forget one thing; it was you who wanted this."

"Yes, I know," I answered, letting my eyes lose themselves along the road. "And if he decides to not join us?"

"Then we will kill him," he said coldly.

I turned towards him; he was serious.

"Even if he is trustworthy?"

"Yes, because it would be too dangerous. Imagine a night of drinking during which our man launches into an incredible story amongst ill-intentioned people, like the vampire hunters. Remember; he knows where we live. Take certain risks to follow your intuition, yes. Do something rash, no."

"I understand, don't worry. I just wanted him to have a choice, now his destiny is in his own hands. I can do no more for him."

"Indeed."

The remainder of the journey to the heliport, the same one we had taken a few months ago to get us to Scotland, was made in silence. I broke it, passing through the security barrier.

"Have you planned anything in particular in Ireland?"

"Yes," he said, parking the car near the hangar where the helicopter was parked.

The door was wide open. Men in overalls were busy around us. I was waiting for more information from Darren, but he just got out of the car after turning off the engine. I stood there open-mouthed, watching him empty the boot.

Moments later, he came to open the door for me, wearing an enormous smile; he knew what I was waiting for, and it amused him not to answer. He would do so of course, but when he wished to.

"Thank you," I replied, smiling too; after all we were about to go on some kind of holiday.

He closed the door behind me and took my hand. We settled in aboard the helicopter, which was finally ready. Ireland wasn't far away, perhaps one and a half hours of flight; it all depended on where he'd decided we would land. I listened to him talking with the heliport's control tower.

"This is flight 9818, flight plan filed, requesting permission to take off."

A click sounded at the end of the sentence, then a voice, nearby but shrouded in static, replied:

"Control tower number two here, you have permission to take off. Be aware of turbulence over the Irish Sea. Nothing else to report. Have a good flight, 9818."

Darren thanked the control tower and engaged various buttons which started the blades of the helicopter revolving. We were alone on the tarmac, the weather was clear for the moment. I couldn't talk to him while he was concentrating on his piloting, I preferred to leave him in peace for the rest of the journey which we still had ahead of us. No turbulence at all disrupted our journey.

I took the opportunity to look at the majesty of the landscape and take some pictures. Darren asked me to reflect on my life, that aspect which I wished to be visible to humans, since it was now clear that I wouldn't be returning to work among them.

I decided that my life would be filled with photography. I wanted to share my passion with humans and others. I didn't think it would make me a living; but at least in the eyes of the world, I had an occupation. I still hadn't discussed it with him.

Our landing destination was Galway; Shannon Airport to be exact. Darren spoke with the local tower control in a more than perfect English, yet I could barely understand the latter, because of his Irish accent. I only really understood the ending *"Failte, flight 9818,"* as this was a word I knew well. We touched down at the place indicated by the air traffic controller. Darren cut the engines, took off his headphones and looked at me.

"Here we are," he said, smiling.

"Yes, and without any turbulence," I added. "We're on holiday: Are you going to tell me now if you have something planned?"

He laughed his head off.

"You're as tenacious as me, you never let it go, do you! You haven't said a word during the journey, and I thank you for that. You took some photographs, which I hope I'll see one day, and then suddenly you come back to your previous question," he finished by saying.

"Well, answer me, then."

"The photos, will I get to see them?"

"Darren!"

He burst out laughing again loudly, while opening the door, and got out without answering my question. I was still watching him with his little game; unloading our luggage, taking it all to a car which was waiting for us, and eventually coming to open the door for me.

"If Madam would care to take the trouble to stand on her ancestors' soil," he said, holding out his hand.

I took his hand.

"I have been here before," I declared.

"I know very well," he paused for a time, and then he added, "but never with me, and believe me; the difference is very important."

I let myself be walked to the car. Darren, who had been a true gentleman since the beginning of our new journey, opened the door, but didn't give me the time to sit down. He pinned me against the car and came up very close to me. I was no longer afraid of him; he put one of his hands on my hips and one on my face. He looked at me with love; he tilted his head forwards and placed a gentle kiss on my lips, which I requited.

"Here is where everything began, Lilly," he said, very seriously.

I gently nodded my head, inviting him to continue.

"The beginning of you... Of me. You were conceived and born here. We were both born here. What's more, I was transformed in this place over a century ago. My ancestors come from this isle and some of yours do too. We'll try to trace your father, perhaps even your father's father. Who knows what awaits us, but we're on this journey together, just you and me, and that's what matters most. We will learn more about ourselves, and discover each other through our histories."

He paused, I had no answer to what he'd just said. I looked at him, just happy to be there, far from all torments. We were together, and the world around seemed so distant to me.

"And to finally answer your question; I have a plan without having one. I landed here in Galway, because there's a large French community in this city. We need to do research, but not only that. We're here, as you pointed out, on holiday; a long holiday which I hope will be fruitful."

He paused for a moment, staring at me.

"Are you okay, Lilly?" he asked, looking worried.

"Yes, I'm very good, don't worry. I'm just a little intoxicated by the place, by your words and by you."

I finished my sentence by resting my head on his shoulder. He squeezed me against him, I could have heard his heart beating.

"We're not done with our emotions yet."

"I know very well; I'll have to save my tears," I said, smiling. "This country has always had a strange effect on me. As if a part of me was left here, just buried somewhere."

"You're Irish; that's normal. Even if you've never lived here, these are your roots. And deep down you can feel it, consciously or not."

"Yes, you're probably right, although these roots come to me only from my father. They are deeply rooted in me, even if I never actually knew him. How will we find him, Darren? I know nothing about him, except for his name and date of birth."

"We have other clues such as the certainty that he married your mother in Ireland. We have information about her. Her name should appear on official documents. We just have to find the starting point. I know a man who can help us find the beginning of the path; following that we'll have to fend for ourselves"

"I'm sure that you know more than one person in Ireland."

He interrupted me by putting his finger to my mouth.

"I said one man; I no longer know anyone else. Everyone I did know has been dead for a long time."

"Who is he then?"

"My aunt's great-grandson, the one who brought me up. Do you remember? I told you about him."

"Yes of course. How will he be able to help us?"

"He works in the town hall at Sligo which is a little way north of Galway. I think he can clarify some points which we're still unsure about, if we haven't already done so."

"You've already spoken to him? You were so sure I would come on this journey!"

"Of course, you know my powers of persuasion," he said jokingly; "but seriously, I sent him an email; he wants to meet us tomorrow at four o'clock."

"A perfect time. What are we doing here until tomorrow?"

"We'll go to Sligo and find a Bed & Breakfast, if you'd like to sleep in a comfortable bed."

My astonished gaze forced him to justify himself.

"For the sake of appearance. You know, we live in a world of humans; we'll leave some traces of having passed through here. And I confess I don't know where to go. Don't forget that we are on holiday, so we'll do as all tourists do in this country; find ourselves a place to sleep, and a place to drink their famous stout."

"Stop it, Darren, I'm teasing you. We're here and we must blend in with the local population, as I well know. As for drinking their beer and dancing a jig, I also agree."

He laughed again and I echoed his euphoria. We were on holiday after all!

An hour later, a sign told us we had reached the town of Sligo.

It wasn't very complicated to find a room with all the necessary comforts, not far from the town, for a very reasonable price; given the fact that we wouldn't be sleeping.

Darren told me he didn't want to call the local vampires at the moment, because he wished us to remain peaceful.

In Dublin, things would be different; he was recognised there as the clan's chief. He therefore would have to greet the community and take the opportunity to introduce me. I dreaded this moment, because it reminded me of my introduction to the family at Peter's birthday party. He told me however, that he wouldn't have to explain himself here.

I was feeling a bit tired somehow; Darren gave me two capsules and suggested that we go to a pub he'd noticed when we arrived. I gladly accepted. I loved pubs and I very much hoped that there would be some musicians present. We went there on foot, the fresh sea air had a very invigorating effect on us. We held hands, feeling free to do so without the family's gaze upon us. I felt light-hearted and happy.

After four months spent away from him, to have him all to myself, and above all here, filled me with immeasurable joy.

There was no live band that night at the pub, but against all expectations the entertainment came from Darren.

He befriended a guy with whom he made a bet; about who could drink more pints of Guinness. Of course, Darren won by a long way, alcohol having no effect on us; but the other guy didn't know that, which made the situation a bit unfair on him. The bet ended around five o'clock in the morning, when the poor man fell flat-out on the floor. Our first night in Ireland had been perfect, although I still wondered why we had rented a room.

Ultimately, it proved very useful for the shower! Darren reeked of beer, even if he wasn't actually drunk, he'd still drank all of them. I stopped counting when he finished his 17th pint, which for me was far too many for a human, or a vampire.

I imagined our first evening together would be a little different, but I'd learned a very important thing about Darren; he had a great deal of humour and he'd been able to play it out tonight.

Next morning, we decided to go for a tour around Sligo's lake; the owner of the Bed & Breakfast having highly recommended some well-hidden places to us, which no tour guide would tell us about.

We had a few hours to kill before our appointment.

3. Marie

The proprietor hadn't misled us, we had in essence come across a "*Holy place.*" Several statues of Saints had been arranged around a cross near a spring, which according to the sign had healing powers. I confined myself to my role as photographer and took some shots, the place was very quiet. Many people were coming to drink and daub themselves with holy water.

Darren didn't stay for long, and walked instead along the edges of the lake. Suddenly, I heard him howl, he turned to face me; within the space of a second he was no longer the same. Approaching him, I could see the fear in his eyes.

"What's the matter?" I asked softly.

I could sense that it was a grave moment.

"We must leave immediately," he told me hurriedly.

I grabbed his arm.

"Tell me what the matter is."

To my great astonishment, he dropped to his knees in front of me. I put my hand on his hair, trying to penetrate his mind. I was able to hear a few snippets of some incoherent thoughts. In turn, I now knelt down and gently lifted his head. I could feel pain, anger, but also and above all, physical suffering. Something had affected him deep down in his heart. However, he wasn't injured, at least not directly.

I looked cautiously all around us; a vampire in a holy place was not a good thing. Then, the glaringly obvious came to my mind: when something happens to a blood brother and moreover a twin, the perception and suffering are multiplied tenfold. I tried an approach that might help him to talk to me.

"Marie?"

He stared at me and huddled himself up. He wasn't crying, he was suffering.

Marie and Albert had moved away after their misadventure in Scotland, they now lived in a small town below Dublin, called Glendalough. They had seemed happy up to now, and yet to judge from Darren's reaction something terrible had come to pass.

"She's not well, I have to help her," he ended up by saying.

"We aren't so far away, let's go."

The advantage of Ireland is that it's small.

I helped him up, taking him by the arm. He'd calmed down a bit, I could only guess that what was happening was seeming to subside. I could understand that perhaps what he was feeling partly toned down his suffering. However, he still hadn't regained his human appearance, and that was a concern. I had never seen him metamorphosed for so long; either he didn't consider it helpful to control it, or he wasn't able to do so. I feared the worst hypothesis.

Arriving at the car, I took the wheel, against his will. He sat himself next to me, I put my hand on his thigh.

"You have to pull yourself together and become human again, please."

"Give me a little time," he said.

The ordeal on the train had shown me that we didn't always know how to manage our transformations, especially in the case of intense stress.

He was trying to contact Marie with his mobile phone, but there was no signal. He entered the coordinates into the sat-nav; we were forty minutes from their home. I started to drive the car immediately and followed the instructions, this wasn't the moment to get lost and hence waste precious time. Darren continued in vain to find a signal.

We could have taken the helicopter, but we didn't have the time to wait for its preparation, and Darren was in no state to pilot it.

He swallowed four capsules, confirming my fear that he hadn't been able to regain his appearance. Despite his age and his experience, certain emotions could touch him to the point that he couldn't control himself. I handed him my sunglasses, which he politely refused. He had found his own at the bottom of the bag.

"It never works when you need it," he said suddenly, throwing his phone on the back seat.

I remained silent to avoid irritating him further. I concentrated on the road, I drove well over the speed limit, trying to make up some time. We didn't possess the gift of stopping time, which I lamented at this precise moment.

"Lilly?"

"Yes, I'm here."

"I am scared," he said finally, after a few seconds.

"Scared that something has happened to Marie?"

"Something has happened to her; I felt it."

"How did you feel it?" I asked, giving him a quick glance.

"A rupture," he replied, leaning back to retrieve his phone.

"What kind of rupture?"

It would have been easier for me to stop the car and have a quiet conversation; he seemed to be calmer now, though his teeth were still visible. He was unsettled.

"Ah! It's ringing..." he said.

I kept my eyes on the road.

"Answer, dammit!"

"Try Albert's number," I suggested.

He looked at me surprised, I knew he didn't have it. I dragged my phone out from my pocket and gave it to him.

"It's his voicemail... Albert, it's Darren; call us back urgently."

Then, he hung up.

A bad premonition began to come over me, there were too many coincidences.

"What kind of rupture, Darren?" I insisted.

"Marie and I are bound by an invisible thread. Whatever the location, we always feel a presence, however small. I had a feeling that something or someone had cut this thread suddenly with scissors. Then..."

He remained thoughtful for a brief instant.

"I had the fleeting vision of Marie lying on the ground." He finished his sentence while looking at the navigation system; there were only fifteen minutes remaining.

I was silent, no words would reassure him.

I continued to follow the directions and left the main road, we were almost there. My anxiety was growing gradually as we delved deeper into the Irish countryside on a dirt road.

"Can you still feel anything?" I ventured to ask.

"No, nothing... nothing at all. We must be very careful Lilly, I don't want any other losses today."

"Don't say that, we still know nothing."

"Me, I know," he whispered.

We were approaching an open gate. The sat-nav announced that we had arrived.

"Park here, please."

I obeyed and parked the car on the side of the road, which had become muddy.

"We will continue on foot, it's more discreet. We must seek and find two bodies."

He said this in a flat tone, without emotion. Darren had felt much more than it had seemed. He had, by all appearances, lost hope: I very much hoped he was mistaken, but I doubt it, alas.

He offered me his hand; like ramblers we passed through the gate. Darren seemed in no hurry now. In other circumstances, I could describe the place as charming, but a tension hung over us that almost prevented me from even thinking.

Nevertheless, here I was, discovering this place. After a few yards, a house came into our view, typically Irish: imposing, made of whitewashed stone and standing two floors high. Marie had put flowers on the various balconies adorning the facade. The house looked big, but not as big as their castle in Scotland, which had been majestic. I was lost in myself assessing this scene, when Darren gently let go of my hand. That's when I sensed a burning smell, which frightened me.

"Wait here, don't you budge," he said. "Okay?"

"Okay."

I watched him walk over to a thin column of smoke which I hadn't noticed beforehand. I didn't want to imagine the origin of fire. My eyes were glued to Darren when a noise behind me caught my attention. I turned slowly around and walked over to a wall, placing my hands gently over it. The idea of what I might discover panicked me. By the time I'd finally discerned what it was, his hand had grabbed mine, making me scream with terror. I leaped over next to him: Albert was alive right in front of me.

"We'll get you out of here," I said, whilst crouched beside him.

I made a quick analysis of the situation: Albert had found himself once again with a stake through the heart, it had become a habit for him; however, not knowing what spell might be linked to it, I refrained from withdrawing it for the time being. The essential thing was that he was alive. I ran my hand gently across his forehead to reassure him, it was black with soot.

"I have to go back to Darren to tell him that you're okay."

I saw a great sadness come over his face, tears were streaming from his eyes. I stood up and looked around for Darren, because he was wrong about one thing: we didn't have two bodies to find, Albert was alive. That gave me a little bit of hope for Marie. Maybe she too had a stake through the heart, and that had cut the connection with Darren: I was hoping it would be so.

I started running, wanting to announce to him at least one piece of good news for today, but I saw him in the distance; his posture immediately made me slow down. He was kneeling in front of the feeble column of smoke. Staring at the scene before him, he was no longer moving. Slowly, I made my way over to him, not wanting to interrupt this moment. It was definitely a moment of reflection. With each and every step, I was more able to distinguish a black figure, which reminded me of the night at the club where a young vampire was sacrificed by humans on a quest of 'de-vampirisation.'

I began to feel Darren's sorrow; the closer I got, the more it overwhelmed me.

He was now a few yards away from me; on his lap I could just make out what was left of Marie's head, with her body still smoking. He surrounded her face with his hands as if to still preserve a little of it, before it reduced to ashes; a final communion with the family ties of the past. I saw his lips move, without understanding his last message to his sister. He looked up at me.

"Would you go in the house and find me a bowl? I want to keep as much ash as possible, she wanted to be buried with my parents."

Then, tenderly he lowered his eyes again to his sister. Anger would come later. Without a word, I turned around and walked into the house. I hadn't been invited in there, but the owner had died; the door opened before me. It was in the dining room that I found a white porcelain pot with a lid. I didn't hang around any longer and re-joined Darren. I placed the temporary urn beneath his hands, he let slip out from between his lips that we were such little beings.

Carefully, he opened his hands, Marie's sweet face collapsed into ashes in the urn. Then he gathered all that he could, filling the pot. For a few moments, he clasped it against him, I didn't dare to disturb him.

"I'm sorry Darren, deeply sorry, my condolences."

"Thanks."

Meticulously, he closed the lid on the temporary urn, which he placed beside him, and began to search the ground for clues. Darren picked up a medallion at the end of a long chain, then stood up and opened it. He froze for several minutes in a heavy silence. I would have liked to tell him that Albert was alive, but did it matter to him at that moment?

"I'm going to have need of you, but later," he said, putting the medallion in his pocket. "For now, we need to clean up and find Albert."

"I've already found him, alive."

I gave him a slight smile. He came over to me and took me in his arms. I felt tremendous sadness emanating from him.

"Why did he not protect her? She didn't have to die that way."

"I know, but I don't have an answer, maybe he tried. We'll ask him, let's go and release him."

I took his hand, but he stopped abruptly.

"Free him?"

"Yes, he has a stake through his heart," I sighed. "Are you coming?"

Arriving at the low wall, a strange feeling came over me. I took a look; Albert was gone. How was this possible? I looked at Darren questioningly.

"He was here, I promise you."

"I believe you, I can sense it."

Worn out, Darren was not responding normally. Nothing in his actions or reactions were normal.

"We would have sensed it if someone had come. Don't you think?"

"He was far enough away from us and hidden by the house. Did you see anything when you went to look for the urn?"

"No, nothing either seen or heard, sorry."

"Stop being sorry Lilly, it's not your fault."

I felt a little bit of irritation in his tone, it was the first time this had happened.

"We need to find him," he added.

With that, his body jerked, as hatred began to come over him. Revenge would be terrible, for the severity of the spectacle before us. I stood there looking at him, his expression scared me.

Suddenly he stiffened, on the alert.

"What happened?" I asked.

"They're here, I sense them not far from here. Concentrate!"

My senses were not yet as sharp as his own; upon concentrating I sensed a different odour, certainly human, but something else too.

"What is it?"

"They have Albert, they had to spray him with a product to mask the smell so that we can't find him. The hunt begins! Stay behind me, be careful and above all, obey me, want you!"

I hardly recognised him. He was someone else, that person I met one night in a doorway in Paris. The same one who made me so scared.

We left, following the fragrant trail that the humans had left behind, taking Albert with them. It took us a few seconds to reach a clearing near the house, in the middle of which was a barn. That the humans were stupid, taking care to cover up the scent of Albert, but not their own, this would lead to their loss. A man stood guard outside the house smoking a cigarette. Darren crouched to the ground, and tugged my arm so that I would do the same.

"I'll take care of him, wait for my signal and come back to join me," he said, whispering, as if someone would be able to hear him at this distance.

I nodded agreement, it only took a fraction of a second before the man collapsed. Darren motioned to me that the path was clear.

"You have to run fast, Lilly, very fast."

"Yes, I know."

I didn't take much longer than him to reach my target. I looked at the fallen man, he hadn't had time to see death coming.

"There are four of them. I'll take care of them, I just want you to watch my back just in case."

He placed his hand on my cheek to reassure me.

"I don't have any choice this time, you understand this, don't you?"

"Yes, I understand, they must pay for what they did. I no longer sense Albert..."

"He's dead now. Stay here."

He pushed the door open sharply, the four individuals turned around, surprised by this intrusion. In a flash, Darren killed three of them, who fell to the floor. I was watching the events through the open door. The last one remained motionless, unable to make a move. I saw a wet trickle running down his trousers. It was high time to be afraid. Softly, Darren approached him, scrutinising him, circling around him. He whispered something in his ear which I couldn't hear; the man began to cry. I found myself smiling at this situation, it was pitiful. I pushed the door and walked over to them.

"Mercy," he begged me.

This was the first time that I had faced a human without hiding my nature.

With no time to react, Darren killed him, but not by breaking his neck. With unprecedented rage he sunk his fangs into his neck, lifting him off the ground. The man was seized with convulsions; when Darren had bled him to death, he threw him away, I heard his body break up against the barn wall.

Darren was staring at me, blood dripping from the corner of his mouth and on his chin. I must have looked scared but I wasn't frightened, I understood what he had done. To me, it didn't change my feelings for him.

Following his gaze, I saw Albert's corpse, in a corner on a pile of straw; I assumed that the humans hadn't completed their task and hadn't had the time to burn him. We made a move at the same moment towards the lifeless body.

"What have they done to him?"

I crouched beside him, his eyes were weird. They were open and yet appeared closed.

"They injected him with silver, he must have suffered terribly," he said closing his eyes.

His eyelids were so stiff, that they made the task difficult.

"It's cruel! Look at his ears, silver is coming out everywhere."

"Yes, I don't understand why they tortured him like this. It's strange, I must admit; maybe they mistook him for someone else."

"What do you mean?"

"I mean, a stake through the heart and burning, that would have been enough to kill him," he said, thoughtfully.

Darren opened his mouth to show me the extent of the damage this poison causes us.

"Now you know what they are capable of."

He got up and continued speaking.

"Humans are like this, and fear makes them stupid and dangerous for us."

I watched him searching for something, and when he picked up a jerry-can of petrol, I understood what he was going to do. He sprinkled all of the bodies except Albert's which he put outside of the barn before lighting a match. The building and its contents quickly caught fire; there was only hay, wood and some poor idiots.

We returned to the house, with Albert in Darren's arms.

"Go into the house. I'll take care of him, he has the right to a decent burial."

"All right."

I had nothing else to say.

Arriving at the house, I turned back towards him and saw him take something from Albert's face, and put it in a small bag, which he put in his pocket. Darren's attitude seemed strange, I put it down to the day's events. I went into the house for the second time, Darren had now occupied himself with Marie's belongings. There was so much here and a large part of it was linked directly to him.

Marie seemed so strong the first time I had faced her. I thought she was invulnerable, but time led me to understand the opposite: at the ball, she showed me her weakness regarding her brother, the episode in Scotland also showed a certain fragility, and now her death. She should have stayed with him; he would have protected her as he had done so well with me.

Moments later, Darren came and joined me. He looked around and realised it would take weeks to tidy up, sort through and take away. He grabbed his phone.

"Martin, I need transport in Ireland."

I couldn't hear how Martin responded, but it was easily imaginable.

"No, not for me, for Marie's and Albert's belongings. We must repatriate it all to the chateau as soon as possible."

There was a silence.

"Thanks Martin, no, I'll do it alone." He glanced at me and corrected himself: "No, with Lilly."

He finished his sentence with a smile to me; this hadn't happened for hours. He hung up, then came over me gently, not wanting to scare me maybe any more than I had already been today. He hugged me up against him, remaining silent for several minutes.

"I didn't want you to experience this. You understand, don't you?"

"Perfectly yes. You can't exclude me from everything, always, and overprotect me otherwise I'll never be able to defend myself. From my perspective, what you have done today is only fair."

"But, you weren't obliged to."

"I wasn't obliged to become a vampire either. Now, there are things I have to come to terms with even if they are not always easy to watch. But at least, I know."

"Yes, now you know what a monster I can be."

I stopped him dead.

"I already knew that, Darren!"

Surprised by my words, he stared at me in silence. He kissed me on my head and looked all around us, here where we had so much to do.

4. Cleaning up.

I was watching Darren, who was trying to sort out Marie's things, but every object, every piece of paper brought back memories for him of precious moments, and especially, that she wasn't here any longer.

We still don't know why all this happened. Marie and Albert lived apart from the world, their rare appearances avoided human contact, and for the most part that of the family of vampires too. They loved to be alone. It was going to really be difficult to work out why, but I knew that Darren wouldn't find peace until he had discovered the truth. Now dead, those men at the barn were only following orders; the truth would come from elsewhere.

As the sun went down, Darren prepared a fire and invited me to come and join him there. A few objects were scattered around him. We closed the shutters, and the doors; soft music by *"Corson"* was echoing around the room.

He seemed to be more relaxed now; I took my place beside him, smiling gently.

"Have you found something interesting?" I asked.

"I don't know. My sister kept so many things that it's difficult to even sort through. Look at this house; it's a veritable museum and yet they only lived here for a short time."

"One amasses a lot of souvenirs over the course of a lifetime, particularly with very long lives such as yours, and you do the same too without realising it."

"You're probably right," he said thoughtfully.

"Then there are also Albert's belongings," I added, as if by apology.

He looked up at me, the reflection of the fire sparkling in his pupils, and he sighed.

"We'll get there, don't worry," I said, trying to encourage him, but this day had been hard.

"Yes, tomorrow Martin's men will come to pack up and repatriate everything to the chateau."

"What shall we do now?"

I wasn't referring to their belongings.

"Find who is behind all this. I want to know why," he said.

He was gently stroking Marie's locket with his thumb.

"I gave this to her a long time ago, she never took it off," he said, without taking his eyes off it.

"It's very beautiful."

Smiling, he handed me the locket. I looked at him, inquisitively.

"Help me, Lilly…"

I didn't understand what he wanted from me. Taking the locket, I questioned him.

"What am I supposed to do?"

"Concentrate, project yourself."

He was facing me, his look passing from the locket to the depths of my eyes, tightening his hands onto mine.

"I have to learn more."

He wanted me to use my gift of retrograde clairvoyance. This gift which I had taken care to go deeper into during my first stay at the chateau. I had taken notes and hadn't stopped reading and learning about it.

"Okay, I'll try," I said softly. "Come and sit behind me, please."

He came as I requested with no questions asked. I grabbed his arms and slid my hands down his to join them together on the locket.

"I've learned a lot about this gift; thanks to this contact which binds us, you're going to experience what I see at the same time as I do. Do you feel ready for this?"

"You're incredible! Did you know that this would be so helpful?"

"No, but I ought to exploit this gift. You said it yourself; it's rare, so I shouldn't waste it. Since you're my progenitor, I'm sure it will work. Shall we start?"

With that, I closed my eyes and was immediately projected to the front porch of the house. It was a beautiful day, Marie was standing a few yards away from me; in the distance I could see Albert, who was busy near the wall; that same one where I would find him a few hours later. She exclaimed, "I'll burn yesterday's rubbish." I instinctively turned my head towards Albert, waiting for his answer. He waved his hand in acknowledgement. Everything was peaceful all around them. I was following Marie from afar when Darren whispered to me, as if someone would have been able to hear us...

"She can't see you; go over to her."

This intervention broke my concentration for a moment: I lost track of time to find myself at the gates of the property. A car was slowly arriving. Some men got out,

I recognised them immediately. I would love to have been able to do something, but it wouldn't have done anything to change the course of history. I could only be the helpless witness in a scenario to which I knew the tragic ending.

Pressing again on the locket brought me back to the fire where Marie was throwing the debris, not suspecting anything. Then everything happened very quickly. I could hear a whistling in the air and Marie collapsed in the midst of the flames, a vision of horror playing out for us. She was immobilised in the fire with a stake thrust through her heart. In her eyes, a last glimmer of helplessness stirred up a mounting anger in me. I turned towards Albert, he was lying on the ground near the wall, unable to move, because they had immobilised him first. Two of the men I recognised came over to Marie.

"Shit! She mustn't die," exclaimed one of the two, watching Marie being consumed in the fire, without doing a thing to help her. But it was already too late.

"We have a contract to fulfil, we'll say that it was just unlucky about her," said the second, a sadistic smile on his lips.

"Yes; the other freak will slaughter us!"

"Don't worry, he'll understand," he finally said, crouching near the smouldering ashes.

I could feel Darren tensing up behind me. Why did he have to go through this? I decided to cut the link. I would have to be gentle with him. I snuggled up against him, pulling his arms tightly around me. I felt him gasping for breath. Waiting until he calmed down, I ventured.

"I have to go further back in time to find out who is behind all this."

After a few moments, a muffled sound came from his mouth. I could feel the icy breath on my neck.

"Yes, you're right."

"Do you want to wait for a little while?"

"No, let's do it, you can carry on again."

I sat up and took hold of the locket again, to find myself a few moments before the car had arrived.

I had learned in the book of gifts, how to go back in time, to define a specific time or location. I had chosen this particular moment because I remembered seeing a man throw something on the ground, and I shouldn't leave anything to chance. The car was approaching us and for the third time on this painful day, the men are dragged out, and one of them throws a piece of paper on the ground. My memory hadn't failed me.

I put the locket back down and explained to Darren that I should go and find this paper, the locket was just showing me the moments of Marie's life; I needed something from one of them, hoping that this man had met the person who organised it. Darren nodded in silence. I got up, took a torch and went out in search of this paper, assuming of course that the wind hadn't blown it away. A few moments later, I was reassured; it was there. I grabbed hold of it too quickly and I immediately found myself projected into a damp, dark place, a cellar perhaps.

I felt a hand being placed on me, which made me jump because it could only have come from the real world. I dropped the piece of paper and came out of my vision.

"Go back inside," Darren told me calmly.

I found myself a little taken aback; I hadn't sensed him following me.

"How did you know?"

"A simple matter of logic," he retorted.

I was after all only a young vampire tapping into a rare gift and not yet fully mastering it.

"Yes of course," I replied.

He picked up the paper. Darren, not having that gift, could pick it up without fear of being projected somewhere else. We resumed our place by the fire, and nestled against him I held out my hand; he put the piece of paper there, which turned out to be a tissue: I was once again projected into the past.

It was indeed a cellar, four men were standing close to each other. A fifth one, on his own meanwhile, stood near a light-well. I couldn't make out his face.

"You heard me very well," he said.

He seemed to be the leader, in any case the others listened to him somewhat fearfully to judge by the charged atmosphere that prevailed there.

"Yes Sir," said a man wearing a cheap red shirt.

"Repeat it back to me if that is the case."

One of them went hesitantly over towards the light-well. He cleared his throat and began.

"We drive to the mansion, there we immobilise the woman without killing her."

"How will you do that?" He interrupted.

"With this wooden stake," said another man, waving a sharp white object.

"And then what?" He continued, putting them under an obvious pressure.

"We immobilise the man and bring him to you at the barn," said the third man.

"This is a simple mission, do you think you can handle it? He said calmly, turning around to add: "Don't do any harm to the girl! Understand?"

It was at that moment that I recognised the organiser, and Darren did too. He jumped up, making me almost fall over backwards.

"I need to breathe, I need air, space..."

He was even more pale than usual. I saw the blood speed up in his veins, striking his eardrums. I joined him on the front steps, he was sitting there with his head in his hands.

"She must not die," he finished off saying.

"No, she shouldn't have," I said, putting my hands on his shoulders as if this gesture could ease his suffering. "Did Albert have some problems? Do you think this is linked with Scotland and the wizards?"

"I don't know."

After a short instant, he added, while getting up:

"I find it hard to think about!"

He was facing me now, his expression had changed. The surprise and the pain had now given way to something else. Something terrible.

"The problem has now come to Alexandre. He is my prey, I will not have peace while he's alive. It matters little to me why he was hunting Albert down, I see only the result: the death of Marie."

I remained silent.

He turned his back to me, losing himself in the darkness.

I was convinced that if he had been alone, he would already be on the way. Alexandre was living on borrowed time, and this had been so from the moment he put his plan into action. How had he even imagined that Darren wouldn't react? Even if Marie had survived, she would have asked for help from the family to avenge Albert's death. I didn't know that vampire; but the two times I had met him, nothing good had come of it.

Slowly, Darren regained his senses. He was walking back and forth along the front steps, moving arms around, as if he was speaking to someone invisible. He finally stopped at the same level as me, but with his back to me. He took his phone and dialled a saved number. Time did not matter to us vampires, we did not sleep; every moment, every second had to be lived through.

"Martin, it's me," he said, suddenly snapping me out of my daydream.

"Yes, the transport will be there at dawn. Darren?"

I realised that, for the first ever time, he had switched on the loudspeaker, sharing the conversation with me.

"I need you to find Alexandre for me."

"Alexandre?"

"He had them killed," he added.

"How can you be so sure?"

"Lilly has the gift of retrograde clairvoyance. We followed the trail back to him. We had heard that Marie was certainly not supposed to die, but she is dead, and in all senses he broke the vampiric law by putting a contract out on the life of another vampire; that of Albert."

"You shouldn't be the one to deal with that yourself Darren, you're much too involved," Martin said quietly.

"I don't give a damn if I'm too involved."

He almost shouted. His anger was palpable on each and every word.

"I have to tell you, it serves no purpose to lose your temper. I'll make enquiries and get back to you. In the meantime, pass me to Lilly."

I was surprised that he asked to speak to me; I came over to Darren.

"Yes?" I replied shyly.

"He must rest. I trust you. Who taught you the subtleties of your gift? I know that Darren doesn't possess this."

"Everything I know I learned in the book of gifts at the chateau. I also tested it successfully in Scotland. I deepened my knowledge, which allowed us today to find our way to Alexandre. Without a shadow of a doubt, he's behind this. Marie is dead, this wasn't intended. They had orders to deliver Albert alive to Alexandre and spare the life of Marie."

Martin remained silent.

"This gift is rare, Lilly," he added.

"Yes, I know, that's why I studied it and refined it further."

"There is one thing I haven't had the time to add in the margins of the book concerning this gift, so I have to tell you now."

"Yes, I'm listening."

"This ability has a drawback: it's exhausting. And this is so to the point that you'll feel the need to sleep."

"But..." I began.

"Listen to me, Lilly."

"Yes forgive me, carry on."

"For this reason, you shouldn't use it when you're alone, because as you know, sleep is a vulnerable time for us."

"Okay. I understand now."

I remained pensive.

"Understand what?" he said worriedly.

"Returning from Scotland, I was convinced of having slept. My eyes were swollen, so I'd slept well. Everything is explained now."

"Yes that's the reason why you'll sleep again on this night. And if needs be..."

"If needs be, what?" I didn't let him finish his sentence, not wanting to hear the rest, which I was dreading.

Darren cut the loudspeaker off, which drove me into a mad rage. I returned to the house and heard him end the conversation.

"I get it, Martin, don't worry. Call me as soon as you get any news please."

Then he hung up to come and join me in the house. He came over to me and wanted to hold me in his arms, but for the first time I pushed him away.

Then finally, I threw myself there.

I understood that it had been for my own good and that we had no need to quarrel especially when it was to do with my health. We stayed entwined for several minutes. Darren carried me to the first floor into a guest bedroom and gently laid me on the bed; my need to rest was now intense. Softly, he placed a kiss on my lips before leaving the room, I was already almost asleep.

The sound of birdsong roused me from my sleep, I felt strange, once again with the feeling of having a bloated face, but now I knew why.

A voice rose up from the ground floor. I hastily got myself up and ready, recognising that it was from my friend Vic. They had arrived now and it filled me with joy. On coming down the stairs, I saw him turn towards me with a big smile; I ran over and leapt into his arms.

"It's been so long, I'm so happy to see you, Vic."

"Careful! You're going to choke me," he said, laughing.

He put me back down on the ground and stared at me, I turned back around on myself to join in his little game, and then stamped my foot.

"Well?" I asked

"You're still so pretty, my little Lilly." Then he held me tightly to him and whispered; "I really missed you. We haven't had much opportunity to see each other since the hostage-taking incident on the train, so here we are; that's put to rights now, so you mustn't leave it so long next time."

"I promise I won't do that again, at least not for so long."

"Allow me to formally introduce you to Philip, I believe he's only here thanks to you."

I turned around and immediately recognised the doctor who I had saved from the train.

"Pleased to meet you, Philip," I said, offering him my hand.

His hand was no hotter than my own; he was no longer human. His decision had been the wisest one, and the only conceivable one if he wanted to remain, so to speak, alive.

"Hello Lilly, I haven't ever thanked you. You didn't give me time, honestly."

"Don't thank me please. I was following my intuition, and apparently I wasn't mistaken since you're here now. So, I don't know whether it's customary to say this; but welcome into the family, Philip."

Behind him, I could make out Darren's silhouette approaching us. I started smiling at him, he didn't seem to have rested much, unlike me. He came directly over and gave me a hug.

"Hello Lilly, how did your night go?"

"Very well, I did sleep and now I'm sure this is no longer a mere impression."

"I didn't know until yesterday evening the side-effects of this gift," he finished by saying.

I smiled by way of a response; after Scotland he hadn't believed me. Martin had the knowledge, he trusted that more than my feelings, even though most of the time he would believe me. He looked closely at me, running his hand through my hair to move it away from my face.

"Martin called me this morning at dawn while you were still asleep. Alexandre is in Belgium. I've contacted the airport; we have permission to take off in three hours from now. Do you think you can be ready?"

"Yes of course. Do you know Belgium?"

"A little, yes. I've already made an appointment with the sheriff of that country; he should be able to help us find him."

Everything was happening very quickly; Darren was determined to wreak his vengeance, but apparently calmly and within the rules. The night and his thoughts had brought him to his senses, obviously.

"And here?" I asked, looking at everything there was to be done.

"Vic will take care of it, don't worry."

"I'll go and get myself ready," I added.

Passing in front of Vic, I put my hand on his arm.

"This didn't last for long, but I'm certain that we'll meet again soon. Take good care of Marie's belongings, he cares a lot about them."

"I know, Lilly; I know this very well," he insisted.

Vic had also been very close to Marie, I'd been tactless because this loss had touched him deeply. I felt at times that I could be selfish. Feeling sad, I returned to my room to gather together the few belongings which I had the time to collect.

A little while later, we travelled back across Ireland, and arrived on time for our flight.

5. Adrian, the Orkani

The flight from Shannon to Charleroi, with a stopover in Paris, went by without any problems and in silence. Darren had remained focused on the sky and I'd been going over yesterday's events in my mind.

I was disappointed to be leaving Ireland so quickly, but I knew that as soon as our task was completed over here, we would be returning. The brief moments of flight over Belgium made me curious about this country; I'd come here to work a few times but never really looked around.

As usual, everything had been well organised; a black Chevrolet Orlando was waiting for us, all we had to do was to load up our things and hit the road. After about thirty minutes, Darren left the E19, we were now no more than eight miles from Brussels. We came to a small town called Beersel, where the information on the road signs was incomprehensible to me. Strange country! I turned to Darren.

"I thought we were going to Brussels," I enquired.

As I finished my sentence, we stopped at the front of a house. Without answering me, he got out of the car, I followed the gestures of his eyes. He opened the post-box outside in order to get the keys, then came back over to me, offering me his hand.

"We'll lodge here for the length of our stay. This house belongs to Vic."

"Is he Belgian?"

"No, but his family has this pied-a-terre here," he finished by adding, without elaborating.

"Okay, that sounds delightful."

He opened the boot, and took out our bags.

Definitely, my bag and I were travelling a lot these days without it so much as weighing me down. I was hoping to be able to do some shopping; I didn't like this very much, but it was becoming more than urgent. Darren had allowed me to take some things like blouses and trousers from Marie's house to tide me over, but I felt I needed to have my own clothing, and moreover, taking his sister's belongings made me uneasy.

I kept back behind him at the front door, which was made of glass and wood in a modern style. It clashed with the front of the house, which was old-style traditional red brick. I imagined that the side and rear of the house had been added over the years as the needs changed.

Opening the door, we found ourselves entering directly into a unique large room. Seen from the outside, there was nothing suggesting such grandeur. I opened my eyes widely as it was so bright and clean. On our right there was a kitchen, followed by a conservatory overlooking a well-maintained garden. On our left was the living room; the furniture was white, together it was all pure and pleasant. This house was tastefully decorated; I put my bag by the entrance and walked into the living room: there was a wood-burning stove in front of a fireplace right next to a wide-screen television. For a simple country house, nothing was missing in this place.

Darren closed the door taking one last glance outside. There were just fields and nature as far as the eye could see. I was surprised, considering we were so close to Brussels.

"Does it please you?" He asked me.

"Yes, it's very beautiful here," I replied. "When will we go to see the sheriff?"

He looked at his watch and answered me.

"In two hours' time, which leaves us a little time to unpack our bags and go, without hurrying."

"For me, that will be a hurry," I began to say.

"I know very well that you have nothing to put on. Believe me the situation pleases me no more than it does you."

He came over and gave me a hug.

"I'd imagined our first holiday together so differently," he said.

"Yes, but this is just a postponement. For now, we have an important thing to do and, believe me, I understand that very well. I didn't know them for very long, but their departure is a big loss and a big void for me too."

"I believe you Lilly, you don't need to justify yourself. I believe you."

He finished his sentence with a gentle smile and kissed me. He was both sad and angry at the same time. These feelings weren't going to be easy to manage.

Upstairs there was a large bedroom, simple yet beautiful. A large iron bed, a white wardrobe and two bedside tables were the only furnishings in this room, illuminated by two large windows overlooking the front of the house. Through these, I could see the car from where I was standing. A quick about-turn revealed the lavatory and a lovely bathroom. Since my transformation, the bathroom had become one of my favourite rooms. I would surrender myself here unashamedly, luxuriating in the water for hours, when my schedule would let me of course. I was lost in my dreams, when Darren told me we had to leave.

We took the road towards the centre of Brussels. The sat-nav showed us the route to follow, we were only twenty minutes from our destination. Darren remained silent: I respected his silence, observing the houses alongside the road, while being jolted by the tram rails beneath the car's wheels. A local radio station was playing a song by "*Serenity*", an Austrian gothic band that I liked very much.

If the reason for our coming here hadn't been so dramatic, I would be able to appreciate it more fully. Somewhere in my head, I made a note that we ought to come back again after we'd been to Ireland.

The architecture of Brussels pleased me very much, there was a subtle blend of old and new. Some streets were lined with trees and with grand mansions. And with these trams appearing from all around, I was happy that Darren was driving. I noticed that he was now looking all around, and that our speed had slowed down.

"Have we arrived?" I asked.

"Yes, I'm looking for a place to park because this neighbourhood is pedestrianised," he said, putting his indicator on.

He put some money in the parking meter, placed the parking ticket prominently on the dashboard, and came over to me.

"I don't know what's going to happen, so stay close to me and be careful."

"Do we have something to fear from them?"

"No not normally, but you never know. Okay?" He asked.

With a nod, I replied in the affirmative. I looked all around us and watched Darren, with his mobile phone in his hand. He was pointing to a small park with some steps.

"It's here, come on."

At the far end of this little square, there was a very strange statue of Béla Bartók, all in black and a little frightening. Then we walked all the way around a building which took us to another square where a market was held. All around the square, there were chocolate shops, each one boasting of the best Belgian chocolate.

I have never liked chocolate.

A maze of streets spread out from this place, we were now immersed in the tourist area of Brussels. There were lots of people all around us. I could hear snatches of conversations in all languages. We committed ourselves to the street that was in front of us; on our right was a long covered alleyway known as *"The Queen's gallery"*. My gaze lingered awhile, and I felt Darren pulling me by the hand.

"Come Lilly, we shouldn't be late."

"Yes, sorry."

I was already regretting my words, feeling the pressure that he was applying to my hand; I let out a small cry barely audible to the average person. I had to toughen up and stop apologizing, this was against my nature, and now I was going to be living with vampires, who for the most part didn't express that sentiment.

The street was narrow; we were startled when suddenly the Grand Place of Brussels opened up before us, in all its majesty. I couldn't help but to stop. Darren gave me an irritated glance, then looked at his watch again; I was about to resume our journey when he came over to me.

"You have five minutes Lilly, not one more," he conceded.

He placed himself behind me, encircling me with his arms, like a lover. I began my visual tour from over to the right: the buildings were very tall, many were ornamented with gold. A pub or a restaurant almost every one of them, except for the City of Brussels Museum, which stood facing the City Hall. On the latter, my eyes alighted for a moment on the highest point, where a gold angel overlooked the city.

Darren whispered in my ear...

"We'll be back, I promise."

Immediately afterwards, we continued on our way, only to come to a stop a few yards further on.

Darren knocked at a heavy wooden door. After waiting a few minutes, which seemed like an eternity, a man opened the door. He looked at us in turn and, without a word, invited us to come in, casting a quick glance outside before closing it. With a wave of his hand, he motioned us to head over towards a door which led us directly into another room. I couldn't feel any tension here. They started talking, in whispers.

I took the opportunity to observe him.

He was one of such beauty; a great purity emanated from him, one might say angelic, but he was made of flesh and bone. I know that the comparison may seem strange for a vampire, but that was the first thought that came into my mind. He had light brown hair; long, very long. His great height served only to exaggerate the length of his ponytail. The colour of his eyes was hard to define, ranging from blue to dark grey. The clarity of his eyebrows and of his skin contrasted his darker eyes. He had a very broad smile, revealing almost perfect teeth. Apparent from his face was a great gentleness, almost innocence. All this and of course the fact that he was a vampire, rendered it impossible to place an age on him, let alone estimate it. But he must have been transformed shortly after the end of his adolescence.

I remained flustered for a moment and then turned around to hide the embarrassment which was beginning to overcome me. I didn't quite understand what was happening. They continued talking without paying attention to my presence, which was perfect.

Darren was invited to come in, I followed on behind him, but the man put his hand gently on my shoulder so that I would understand I wasn't invited. He pointed to a chair near the window, politely adding: "Please." Darren turned to me; his look told me that I had nothing to fear.

I looked up towards the one I would now describe as a guard.

"Very well then!" I said, resignedly.

The door closed upon Darren; I found myself almost alone. For a moment, I tried to listen to what was being said in the other room, but I could hear nothing. So I started to look all around me. The room was circular, the walls covered in an ochre paint. A golden moulding marked the border to the ceiling, which was also ornamented in the middle by another moulding, this one being round. This narrowed the room, making it seem a little oppressive. There were three doors; the one by which we had entered, the one that Darren had used a few moments earlier, and a last one which remained a mystery.

Despite its proximity to the Grand Place, which was full of people, this place was silent. I was hoping once again that we would have time to look around a little, but that all depended on what was being discussed in the other room, where I hadn't been allowed to go. But Darren had promised to do so: sooner or later I would get to know this city.

I left my inner thoughts and now my gaze fell again upon the guard. He was still standing near the door. Was he protecting the sheriff who Darren had come to see?

I got up and looked out through the only window in this room. People outside were walking, laughing, just simply living. I envied them somehow.

"Their happiness is short-lived, as are their lives."

I turned to face him; he was now standing two or three yards away from me. His look was disturbing.

"I know," I replied, throwing them one last glance.

I took advantage of the fact that he'd started the conversation to attempt to find out a little more. But even before I'd opened my mouth, he began to speak.

"I sincerely believe that she can help, and her name is Lorelei, but nowadays she's called Lou," he said, smiling.

"You don't have the right," I began protesting. "The sheriff is a woman?"

"I've more right than you can imagine Lilly. Yes, she's a woman. Are you jealous?"

I frowned.

"Not at all, just surprised. Why couldn't I accompany Darren?"

"Martin requested an interview for him; we knew he would be accompanied, but this doesn't however give you the right to enter. Does it bother you that I'm calling you 'Lilly'?"

"It's a little late to ask, I think."

Contrary to all expectations, he approached me and offered me his hand.

"Adrian."

I hesitated for a moment, then took his hand. This gesture was so human to me. In recent months, I had avoided this kind of physical contact with humans because of the coldness of my skin. It was a cautionary rule.

"Enchanted," I said politely.

"Don't be wary of me, or of us; Belgium's vampires. We're very familiar with your family and like to work in the same manner as you."

"But me, I don't know you," I added.

I remembered Darren's words. He'd told me to stay on my guard and that's what I was doing.

He took a chair and sat astride it in front of me, I instinctively stepped back. I stared at him, this vampire was strange; cold, but endearing. I realized now that I was smiling.

"Do you know where we can find Alexandre?"

"That's not a question I can answer," he said, placing his hands on his knees. "Lilly you are young, very young; a baby to me. Don't be so impatient. Darren will come out of that room with all the information needed to help you find the person or persons who are responsible for Marie's and Albert's death, and those who violated vampire law."

"You knew full well that I would come, since you already know my name, so what's the real reason that I can't attend this meeting? We would have gained some time, Darren and I."

"Lou asked me to let only him enter."

"I guess that if I were to ask you why, you wouldn't tell me."

"Indeed."

"And do you know why?"

"Of course."

He got up, and stared at me very seriously: in that precise moment, he no longer seemed angelic.

"There are hierarchies to respect here, Lou is our sheriff here in Belgium. Not only to our family, but to all Belgian vampires. There is one in each country, and some have even more like in Canada, Russia or even France."

"Who are they in France?"

He looked at me in surprise and came back to sit down in front of me, but this time in a normal fashion, which gave the conversation a little more formal turn.

"You really don't know?"

Since I remained silent, he rightly concluded that I was being serious, and then continued.

"I think you need a little lesson in vampire politics."

"I hate politics," I said, with a snort.

"Would you like to know, yes or no?"

"Yes, I'm listening."

"In France, you have three sheriffs. The first is Martin, who you know. He's the most powerful. He looks after the South-eastern part, which runs from Clermont-Ferrand to the border of Switzerland and down to Corsica. This also includes the Mediterranean coast, you see?" He asked.

"Yes, absolutely."

"The second sheriff is Eddy," he began... "Who, by all appearances, you don't know! Eddy Viars, he manages an area extending from the top of Brittany to the Spanish border, limited widthways over to Clermont. And finally, your dear and secretive Darren."

"Darren is a sheriff?" I asked, taken aback.

"Yes, in the North. Did you never ask the question when he took himself away to Italy?"

"No," I said pensively. "He told me that it was a meeting of clan leaders. I didn't need to know more. How do you know?"

"I know all Lilly, I've told you," he added. "But things have changed; you came back to live with the vampires. Darren didn't have to give you any details at the time since your transformation was... how do you call it?"

"Therapeutic."

"Therapeutic, yes," he repeated, as if to convince himself. "So a sheriff receives other sheriffs and they recount tales about..."

"Sheriffs," I added, laughing, but still pensive.

"So there you are: you now understand why you're not invited in that room."

"You're what or who exactly? Excuse my clumsiness, but..."

"No, don't apologise, it's a legitimate question. I'm an Orkani."

A moment of silence invited him to continue.

"I am a keeper of knowledge and possessor of very rare gifts. We don't choose to be Orkani, we are *"born"* like this."

"But we're not born vampires actually!" I exclaimed.

"Some are, but that's another story. It was on my second birth that my special nature was discovered."

"I haven't read anything like that in the book of gifts."

"Artur's book of gifts deals only with actual gifts. To be Orkani is not strictly a gift as such, but rather a condition. But also a godsend, without wanting to play on words," he added, giving me a wink.

He amused me while he was teaching me.

Adrian now went on to steer the course of the conversation.

"Why were you perusing that book?"

"I was looking for information on retrograde clairvoyance."

He nodded.

"Would you like me to tell you more about Orkanis or should I enquire about a book on the subject?"

He smiled at my reflection.

"Curiosity is well developed in you, Lilly."

Just as he was about to tell me more, the door opened. They had apparently finished. I got up to go and join Darren. I saw the sheriff for the first time; she was a very beautiful woman, not because she was a vampire, but because she had been beautiful as a human. She had very delicate features, her hair was short and blonde. She smiled at me and gave me a nod, before giving Darren a friendly kiss and retiring to her chambers.

Without saying a word, Adrian accompanied us to the door, then turned around to me and said:

"You'll have to come back again, unless you find some answers in the depths of your soul, Lilly."

Then he bid us goodbye. I watched him close the door, not comprehending this last remark.

"What did he mean by that?"

"I don't know."

"Darren, what's happening?"

He stared at me strangely.

"What did the sheriff say?"

"Everything will be okay, Lilly; come over here by me."

"Why?"

At that very moment, everything became black all around me, and everything began to dance around. Once again, powerless over what was happening to me, I fell into   Darren's   arms.

6. A Truth

Lying on the bed, trying to regain some strength, I realised once again that my body had let me down. How was this possible, and why? I was exhausted, which for a vampire, even a young one, was abnormal.

I looked at Darren and Martin, they seemed just as worried as I was, what was the matter with me? And why was Martin here? And for how long?

"Why is she so weak, Martin?"

"I still can't explain it at this point."

He remained pensive for a moment.

"It's the third time this has happened since you've transformed her, isn't it?"

"No, the second time," he replied, frowning.

"I believe the episode on the train was another weakness than simply lack of food."

"What are you thinking?"

"I'm not sure. Let's recap. Lilly came into the club for the first time, in the search for a vampire, at the end of last summer. Following that, the transformation occurred in two phases; a rare thing, but not unlikely since there are already precedents for that."

"Yes, we put that weakness down to her human physical condition."

"Yes... Yes. Then she caught a cold, and once again you had to feed her so that she could recover. Correct?"

"Uh, yes. Where are you going with this, Martin? You're starting to worry me."

I was listening to them, still half asleep.

With his arms crossed, Martin was standing over by the window, he was running his hand across his chin while thinking aloud. Darren was standing behind him, without taking his eyes off him.

"So, there have been three occasions now, in less than a year, when Lilly has needed vampire blood to regenerate herself."

"And?"

"It's interesting... What do you know about her, Darren?" He asked, throwing me a glance as he turned towards him.

"No more than you do; our trip to Ireland would have allowed us to find her father, but for the reasons which you know, we came here."

"And her; what does she know about herself?"

"She vaguely told me about her mother. I know nothing more," he said, disappointedly. "I was only intending to transform her, and then follow her from afar, by way of a progenitor. The contract was to end there."

"Yes I know, and you didn't know you would become more attached than you'd planned."

"Actually, I like her very much, Martin. But would you care to tell me why you have all these questions?"

"I'm still thinking about it," he said, finally.

He headed over to me, while still addressing Darren.

"Help me to turn her on one side please."

"What are you going to do to her?" Darren enquired, also coming over to me.

I let them turn me over; I had no strength left and I wanted to save what little there was in order that I might continue listening to them: I wanted to know what was happening.

"I need to check something, roll her trousers up as far as her knee, her right leg," he said, kneeling at the foot of the bed

Darren complied and gently rolled back my trouser-leg above my knee: I didn't understand a word about what he was seeking. I could feel Martin's breath, while he was observing the back of my knee; I felt his fingers resting on my skin. What was he looking for?

"Look," said Martin, a hint of excitement in his voice.

He got up, allowing more room for Darren, who in turn knelt behind me.

"What should I be seeing?"

He leaned in closer.

"But..."

"You know the significance of this?"

I could now feel Darren's fingers drawing a circle on my skin, a circle with a line through it: I had no idea what that meant, but it seemed important in the eyes of Martin.

"Yes, I've heard of this mark before, but it's so rare that it barely exists, if at all. What's the probability of her being an "Im...?" Darren tried to pronounce it.

"An Imhumvamp! You don't need to be afraid to say it. And this now explains lots of things you see. Why hadn't I thought of it before? I'm an imbecile!" He exclaimed, slapping his forehead with the palm of his hand.

So Martin was now in a state of total excitement; as for Darren, he continued touching the mark, which I'd never noticed before, in the crook of my knee.

"How doesn't she know it herself? I don't understand," he finished by saying, whilst rolling the leg of my trousers back down again.

I gave a hint of a smile, which I couldn't explain. A strange feeling of serenity overcame my mind and I felt my body become calm.

"She's a part of the fundamental roots of our race and she doesn't know it, not consciously anyway. This is their means of protecting themselves."

"Explain it to me Martin," intervened Darren, sitting on the edge of the bed, a hand placed on my foot.

The doctor sat on the window-sill and began his tale.

"A very long time ago, many centuries ago to be more precise, a family of poor Irish farmers were living reclusively in the county of Kerry. There were fifteen children, some say more, but not all of them were the same. Ten of them were born with what they believed at that time to be a congenital defect. They were very often sick and weak, but they were endowed with an uncommon propensity which saved them: they ate very little except blood; their own blood! They would bite and drink between each other, and they quickly realised once they reached adulthood, that they were no longer physically ageing. The ten children sustained one another; they were very close, for all intents and purposes inseparable. They said goodbye to their family and friends, and began to disperse themselves around the world a bit; but always in pairs so they could continue feeding, for the one and only thing which satiated them was their own blood That was until one of them, Armon, finding himself caught up in a bad situation, had to feed on the blood of a human; and thus was born the first vampire of their descendants.

Because after that bite the human survived, but he had been changed; he had become like Armon, a bloodsucker, and thus an inexhaustible source of nourishment for him. Armon promptly let the other family members know that it was possible to extend their family with a simple bite. And so that was the beginning of our history. But Imhumvamps had, and still have, a faculty which we other *"common"* vampires don't."

Martin stopped to catch his breath. Darren was hanging on every word of his story. As for me, certain memories were coming into my mind.

"If over a period of time they don't feed on vampire blood, they become a kind of human possessing immortality. They also lose certain notions about time or memory. Then they become more and more feeble, until their instincts surface again; and hence one of them, such as Lilly, crosses the threshold of our club. Since their thirst becomes unbearable, somewhere within them, the need to be what they've always been, without them really being conscious of this during their human phase, reappears."

"But she should be able to remember now," Darren interjected.

"No, because they need time. We don't know how long Lilly's been *"hibernating"*. The only thing we know now," he looked down at me "is that she's very old, even though she doesn't appear so. And we now know why she possesses so many gifts which seem so simple for her."

Martin stood up to take a better look outside; the sound of car having attracted his attention. He continued his story.

"This hibernation has enabled them to survive over the centuries, this strategy is what saved them from the exterminations of vampires, which were burnt at the stake, in the early 18th century: they were human in the eyes of all. The sole thing which authenticates them is on the back of their knee: a circle with a line through it; those ten children have this birthmark."

"How do you know this, Martin?" Darren asked curiously.

"I know most of them, but one in particular taught me a lot before retiring to the mountains of Tibet."

"Artur Mills?"

"Indeed Darren," he said, smiling.

"Lilly had the book of gifts in her hands, she studied it without ever sensing that it had been written by her own brother!"

"This book has passed through many hands, and he wrote it so long ago. But then don't forget that at that time, as we know now, she was reviving!"

"How long will it take for her to remember everything?"

"I don't have all the answers. Who owns the car which is parked just outside the house?"

Immediately, Darren took a look and then turned back to me.

"It's the neighbour's," he replied, coming over to sit next to me.

I smiled at him tenderly, not knowing what to think myself. I imagined him to be lost with what he'd learned, at least as much as I was. He responded to my smile.

"How are you feeling?"

"Lost, but this will get better soon."

I sat up in bed and whispered to him:

"This doesn't change anything, does it?"

"Change what?"

"Your feelings for me."

I stared at him, I needed to know.

"Of course not," he said, taking my head in his hands.

He stared at me for a moment; I could see that he was telling the truth. Then he kissed my lips, which I requited.

"I imagine we no longer need to go to Ireland to find my father. However, I'd still like to take that journey with you, because that's still where it all began."

"Yes, you're much more Irish than we imagined. And much older too," he added, chuckling.

"Martin?" I called out.

"Yes," he replied, pulling himself away from what was happening outside.

"Who is the woman who passes herself off as my mother?"

"She's what's commonly known as a chaperone. Imhumvamps need someone to watch over them during their human phase. Soon, the memories will come back to you, and you'll be able to answer all your questions and ours too, at the same time."

"You shouldn't change your attitude towards me. I am and still remain Lilly; the unique therapeutic vampire."

"For the others yes, you'll remain our therapeutic vampire. But know that for us it will be a little different, because some vampires don't like Imhumvamps, and some would like to study them in detail in order to reproduce this gene which makes you special, more so than just being the originals."

"And?"

"We will protect you differently."

"Which is to say?"

"Lilly, you're the one who'll survive. You, your brothers and sisters, immortals among mortals defying the centuries. If tomorrow all of us disappear, "You", you'll still be here. You are the guardians of our race, permitting our continuation, or our eternal new beginning. You are our genes, our hopes of survival," said Martin, on a solemn tone.

"Where are my brothers and sisters?"

As far back as I could remember, I'd been an only child; and I suddenly rediscovered myself as part of a family of ten children.

"They could be anywhere. We have no way to identify you other than this birthmark, and of course a few clues like those which led me to think that maybe you might be one of them."

"When I've recovered all my strength so to speak, will I have the possibility of sensing the others?"

"When that does happen, your memories will come back to you, along with your abilities and your answers. Since, look; you've all survived so far to my knowledge, by grace of this ability of yours to blend into the crowd, passing through the centuries without getting discovered by anyone. And of course keeping it secret about what you are."

"I really can't die?"

"Yes, there is one way. Artur confided this secret to me on a day of great loneliness. He revealed it to me in case he wanted to really end it all."

"What way is that?" I asked, raising myself up on the bed.

"Silver," he answered, simply.

"Silver, but we all know that's harmful to vampires."

"Harmful, yes, as it burns our skin, but we heal ourselves very quickly. There exists a little-known punishment that's fatal for you: which to pump your body full of silver. This isn't a common execution, the vampire hunters being content with a stake through the heart and with fire. They don't even know about this method. Only a few people are aware of the means to inflict this ultimate death."

I looked at Darren, who went pale, as did I.

"What are you concealing from me, you two?" Asked Martin.

I remembered that this very act had shocked Darren.

"Albert was killed in just this manner," Darren ended up saying.

"Does this mean that Albert was my brother?" I asked.

"There's one way to make sure. But why would Alexandre have wanted to kill one of you? You're not a threat, you're just the origins of our race and the preservers of our genes. That death is illogical."

Martin was pacing around the room; too many unanswered questions were coming into his mind. Suddenly, he turned around to face us.

"I must go to Ireland; I have to see the body. As for you two, you stay here. And find me Alexandre!"

He came over to me and said, fixing me in his gaze:

"You should feed yourself with vampire blood to recover all your strength; the sooner the better for you, and for all of us. We'll know very quickly whether he was indeed your brother or not. I'm leaving right at this very moment."

He turned to Darren.

"Do whatever you have to do."

Then he left the room without any further hesitation.

Suddenly we found ourselves alone, and feeling somewhat disconcerted. Darren came over to me and whispered:

"You heard what he said. Feed yourself from me, Lilly."

I felt bizarre, as if something had become liberated inside me. I stared at him and felt no guilt about the idea of biting him. More than that though, I yearned for him to touch me, discover me and become intoxicated in my hidden aromas. I drew my open mouth up to meet his. I inhaled his breath without touching his lips, and then descended the length of his neck, where I placed a kiss. My whole body was starting to boil. I ran my tongue along my lips, staring at his carotid artery, and placed my fingers on it. I stroked this artery, which was now swollen with excitement, feeling his blood circulating and calling to me. I moved in closer and closer, and touched his skin with my mouth. I placed another kiss there, and suddenly I could no longer hold myself back; I sunk my teeth into his neck and felt him flinch. His blood rushed into my body, nourishing me with what was vital for me; vampire blood!

Gently, he pulled himself away from my grasp and looked me straight in the eye. Blood was dripping from my mouth; he tilted his head with a strange look in his eye. I felt the tip of his fingers run along the stream of blood; I opened my mouth again, to let him introduce his fingers, delighting in this last taste of sweet nectar.

I could no longer recognise myself, a furious passion overwhelmed me. Was this because of his blood, himself, or both of these?

"Show me," I whispered to him.

"Show you what?"

"The passion that you have for me.

I did see this passion in his eyes, I felt it in the tips of his fingers and in his kisses. Nothing else mattered right now except us. We spent the night together, to deepen what we had merely skimmed over for months, without ever acting on.

In the morning, feeling blissful, I was daydreaming among my very many questions. Nothing was really clear yet about who I was. I vaguely understood the importance of protecting myself, since I myself now had the means to do it. Or perhaps there was something Martin was hiding from me.

Still, I felt very well. I no longer felt that fatigue, and the all the less so every time I fed myself from Darren. The capsules weren't going to suffice in the medium-term.

Vampire blood was my food.

So I wasn't a predator, but one of the origins of our race.

I was much more vampire than I had known or believed. Now it was my duty to remember everything, I felt this deep down inside me. Perhaps Adrian would know the way to bring my centuries of existence back to the surface. Perhaps so...

Darren turned to me.

"You'll find the answers, Lilly."

I looked at him fondly.

"I know. This all now explains why I couldn't be satisfied with my human life. It makes sense. All my weaknesses, all my years of suffering were because I was only a mere part of myself. The danger would have to have been big for me to feel the need to go through that. What's more, I'm convinced that this isn't the first time I've hibernated, in the words of Martin. And that this suffering would be the same each and every time, when it manifests itself, this is the trigger for my return among the vampires."

"You have a strange way of saying it or feeling it, but this is apparently the way you function."

A very strange survival instinct which leads to a death.

Darren got up in order to take a shower, I didn't take my eyes off him until he left my field of vision. Things would come back to me little by little; I certainly didn't expect to relive those centuries of existence, but to remember would be good for me.

Up until this day, how many times must I have had to remember it all?

I went to back to sleep again, peacefully

7. My Family

A few hours later, I woke up; a quick glance led me to understand that I was alone. I could no longer feel Darren's presence. In less time than it takes to even say the words, I found myself downstairs. An envelope was lying on the worktop near the coffee machine. I opened it.

"My dear Lilly,
Excuse me for going away so quickly and leaving you on your own, but due to recent events, I can't and don't want to risk bringing you along.
We haven't had time yet to talk about my meeting with Lou. Alexandre is in Austria, in Vienna. I have to find him and bring him back before he moves on again. I don't want to lose another moment and thus squander any chances of capturing him. He must face judgement.
I left you some of my blood in the fridge.
I would advise you not to leave the house, but knowing you, I realise you won't follow this recommendation, however wise. So my guess is that you'll

be heading to the only destination you know in Brussels. I've put Lou's house number into your phone and I let her know about your potential call.

I will keep forever in my memory, the night which we just spent together.

Forgive me, I love you,
Darren."

I stayed pensive awhile after reading this letter. Darren had changed his attitude towards me, as if I'd suddenly grown up.

I wish he would have taken me along.

The love which he had for me protected me always, but now he knew that I could take care of myself, like I'd done through the centuries. When we'd been at the chateau, he'd been angry about my escapade to the nearby village, which hadn't even lasted one hour. And now he'd left me alone in an unknown country. He knew more about me than he was letting on. But above all he had confidence in me.

Not knowing how long Darren would be away, I just drank a quarter of the bottle of blood, which was already much more than all the other days, except of course for the last two.

I called a taxi, because he was right of course; I didn't intend to stay here and wait quietly. In the meantime, I got myself ready.

Ten minutes later, I told him that the historic centre was my destination.

Forty minutes passed by before I recognised the black statue of Béla Bartók, still scary to my eyes.

I'd brought my camera along, and appeared to be the perfect tourist.

The market was in full swing in the square; this time I'd have time to stroll around. Stalls were selling mainly handicrafts, jewellery and paintings. Twenty or so small wooden stalls were dotted around and the place was swarming with people.

I took pictures of everything and anything, I liked doing it this way because a few photos would always come out a bit different, thanks to a detail, a colour, an object or a face. The people's expressions, which don't always call out to me at the time of shooting, sometimes give me some nice surprises when I look back at them later.

The weather here was beautiful. I was feeling good, this hadn't been the case for a long time now. Apart from missing Darren, this afternoon was almost perfect. I sent him a text message to tell him that I loved him and that I was in Brussels.

I'd taken the same route as a few days beforehand; now an aroma caught my attention. I closed my eyes, motionless in the middle of the crowd, and let myself penetrate into it; it was gentle and sweet, bringing back memories of times long past. I slowly opened my eyes again, noticing that to my right there was a sweet-shop, which was probably closed last time.

I went inside, it was colourful and soft in there, but at the same time tangy and warm. Spread before me were dozens of jars containing all sorts of candies: gums, multi-coloured marshmallows, toffees both flavoured and natural, and all number of other sweets. I was in a children's paradise, and I joined in the game by preparing myself an assortment that I would never savour; but I wanted to bring that aroma away with me.

The cost was hefty, I may have overdone it, but this didn't matter much, because I was feeling good.

A few yards further on, I found myself at the Grand Place; this time I would be able to appreciate its real qualities. Seating myself on the terrace of one of its many cafes, in the shade of an umbrella, I ordered a beer.

I was studying the angel which overlooks the city, using the zoom lens on my camera, when I felt a hand on my shoulder. What I felt at that precise moment filled me with serenity. Something had changed in me. I gently put the camera down on the table and turned around.

"Ah! Hello Adrian! How did you know I would be here?"

He slid his phone over to me, smiling. I looked at him, then looked down at the screen: '*She is in Brussels, protect her please. Darren.*' I pushed the phone back over to him. Darren hadn't wasted any time.

"May I offer you something to drink?"

"I'll have the same as you, thanks."

I motioned to the waiter for him to bring us another beer, which he did as quickly as he could.

I was looking at Adrian without knowing why his face fascinated me so much.

"How did you find me? Am I that predictable?" I asked, looking him in the eye.

"Your specific scent led me to you. And may I remind you that I live on just the other side of the square; it was not really so hard to smell you!" He added.

"Can you smell all - I lowered the level of my voice and drew closer to him - vampires?"

"No, of course not. If that were the case, it would distort my sense of smell. I have the ability to detect them all, you too I might add, or any other vampire for that matter; but I do only smell a few. Those closest to me like Lou for example or those who give off a different scent, like you.

"How am I so different?"

I stared at him again, I wanted to know if he was lying.

"You know very well the answer. Only since recently of course, but now you know it," he said, leaning back in his seat.

"And how is it that you know I'm different, if in fact this is the case?"

"Didn't I tell you I knew more things than you might imagine?"

"That's an easy answer, don't you think?"

It seemed as if we were playing a game of cat and mouse.

"It's just the truth."

He paused awhile, drinking a little beer. Then he put his elbows on the table. He looked right into my eyes and continued talking very seriously.

"Your scent is different, but it is the same as other people that I know. In addition, your aura is radiant, so to speak. You aren't just a common vampire."

"How come?"

I had to know whether he really knew, or whether he was playing with a lie in order to discover the truth.

"Okay," he said, sighing. "As you seem to doubt me yet again. I'll tell you what you are. You're an Imhumvamp, which is to say, one of the ten descendants of Lilith. Five girls and five boys. You are the origin of our race and our genes. Will this do for you?"

"Yes, it's a little sketchy, but I'll be content with it," I replied. "I still have some memory lapses you know."

"I don't doubt that for a moment. The last time I lost track of you, it was 1982; you were in France, in Paris to be precise. So that's 31 years ago. Incidentally, the older things will come back into your memory first. This will help you to know who you are. It's all part of the process."

"How do you know that?"

"Lou is your sister and my progenitor. So whatever she knows, I know too. She's also one of the rare few, perhaps the only one, who has ever been only a vampire."

"Why?"

"She is the strongest of all of you."

"Why didn't she say something, nor even you for that matter, when we first met?"

"Would you have believed her?"

"No, of course not."

"You see, you can find the answers on your own, like an expert."

"We could say that you're helping me to find them," I said, smiling.

"That's not untrue, I do admit."

I looked all around us, no one was paying any attention to two people sitting on a cafe terrace chatting over a drink. The place was packed with people. I carried on talking to him whilst observing everything around us.

"Is it because she's your progenitor that you're Orkani?" I asked, resting my gaze on him.

"No, not at all. But because I am an Orkani, she keeps me close beside her. She educated me, showed me the way to find out who I was."

"Were you a willing vampire?"

My question obviously embarrassed him; he took his time to respond.

"I was dying. Do you think I had a choice?"

I felt pain in his voice, but no regrets.

"Apparently not. How did it happen?"

"There was an attack... As was often the case, but on this occasion we didn't have the time to take refuge in caves. The people of the north could be cruel. They killed my whole family before my eyes. Without exception; my mother, my brothers and sisters, all beheaded. I don't know for what reason they decided instead to hang me, but in their haste they hadn't noticed that the very ends of my feet were touching the ground, not much I must say though, but just enough to keep me alive."

He took another sip of beer, a longer one this time. I respected his silence, he needed it. Then he continued.

"Before that, they had tortured me; my mutilated body was just asking to die. I had suffered terribly."

He looked me in the eye before continuing; he wanted me to understand his story well. I stayed silent, still without breaking his gaze. Along with him, I would now have to face this which I'd asked him about.

At that moment, he took hold of my hands and transported me to the exact moment of his torture. I could see it through his eyes; I could feel, through his body, the suffering that he had endured.

I was hanging right there with him, his bruised body just begging to die. It was raining when I saw her, dressed in a blue robe, mounted on a black horse; a very tall one, perhaps a thoroughbred. Nothing seemed to affect her; neither rain nor the devastation all around. She was heading straight to Adrian and to me. She dismounted from her horse. How beautiful she was! She touched a hand to my leg and sensed life, then delicately she took me down from there and lay me on the ground. She assessed my condition, each of her touches making me feel worse. She leaned over to me and I saw her teeth.

"I can cut short your suffering and give you eternal life," she whispered to me.

I wasn't able to answer, I was dying. I was so frightened by what she was.

"If you want this, squeeze my hand," she said.

She took hold of my hand, this rare part of my body without any wounds. I was still staring at her, beauty overwhelmed me. I gave her a slight pressure, giving her my consent, not really knowing what it meant.

"One last thing my little one... Vengeance should not be part of your life. You'll forget all this and bear no grudges, rancour has no place in my world. Are you still alright with this?"

A second squeeze gave her that agreement which would change my life, her life.

"Very well," she said, softly.

She finished her sentence and threw herself on top of me, planting her teeth into my neck, depriving me of my last human breath, the last of my pain.

Adrian let go of my hands now; the scene instantly vanished from my vision, I was back again in the Grand Place in Brussels in the 21st century.

"This procedure has more value than just words, I hope you didn't mind, Lilly?"

"No, not at all. I better understand your devotion to her now."

"It's more respect than devotion, she's everything to me."

"Why did I feel all of that? I thought retrograde clairvoyance could only show us things. Back there, I was suffering when you were suffering, I squeezed her hand when you wanted to. How is this possible?"

"It's the fusion of gifts which allows us to do that."

"And what if... I hadn't squeezed her hand?"

"We can't change the past, Lilly; we can only see it or experience it, but in any case we can't influence it."

He stood up and held his hand out to me.

"Come with me, please. I'll show you something that will help you to come back among us a little more quickly."

"Back among you?"

"Yes, to remember who you really are."

I stood up and followed him.

A few paces were all it took to bring us to the door of the Lou's house, my sister. This time, we were going upstairs. It was very different from the confined space of the room the last time.

This one was large, very sparsely furnished, but on the other hand these walls were lined with various tables. I followed Adrian who headed over to a large fresco, though I was wondering about one thing.

"Where is Lou?"

He turned to me, a little embarrassed.

"With Darren."

This reply was disconcerting to me, because he hadn't wanted me there.

"For what reason? He wrote a note to tell me he had to leave immediately, and to say that he couldn't take me along for fear of Alexandre fleeing again."

"Lou didn't want him to go alone for various reasons. The first being that Darren can be impulsive and might want to kill Alexandre when he should instead face judgement. The second is that Alexandre is your brother, and we need to know why he killed Albert, who was also your brother. Thus, as it appears to be a family affair, Lou went along with him. Against his will, if that makes you feel any better.

"Alexandre is my brother... and Albert too. This doesn't make any sense!"

I continued to think about this accumulation of new information concerning my family.

"Yes indeed, it makes no sense, so therefore we need to know about it. Coming back to our subject, if you please Lilly."

"Uh... Yes, okay."

I was still standing in front of the fresco, but without really looking at it; the situation perturbed me.

"You don't have to worry, Lilly," said Adrian.

I smiled half-heartedly. He put his hand on my shoulder which had the effect of relaxing me.

"Look, here is your family in all its glory, at least the vampire part."

"Where's my father?"

I could only see my brothers and sisters, alongside my mother in this picture, finding this to be strange for a whole family.

"Your father wasn't a vampire, only your mother gave you the gene."

"But she wasn't a vampire herself, is that right?"

"It's a bit more complicated than that. Come back to this for the moment; don't go too fast Lilly, otherwise you'll confuse yourself, and that's not good in a cycle of Recouvrance."

"A cycle of Recouvrance?"

"Yes, when you're reborn as you have now been. When your memories come back and overwhelm you."

He pointed out to me every person present.

"Here on the right, this is Laura. She lives in a convent in Spain, she's very strange."

"I don't doubt it for a moment... to live in a convent! How does she feed herself?"

"She's human for the moment."

"Ah! Okay."

"Next you have Lou here, who you must certainly recognise despite the long hair. And there, next to her is you."

I came up closer in order to get a better look at myself.

"Are you sure? I don't recognise myself."

"This fresco is centuries old," he laughed, "I recognise you. You had a pretty pink dress I must say!"

I pushed him to the side, giggling.

"Don't you like pink any more, perhaps?"

"I've never liked pink, it must have been my mother! Carry on instead of dwelling on my wardrobe."

"Okay, so here's Lizzy, depicted here pointing her finger; she lives in London with a charming vampire called Humphrey. And the youngest one is Lusiana, who lives in Germany in a clan of vampires. That could be one reason why Alexandre is in Austria, they are very close. Are you following me so far?"

"Yes, very well, thanks."

I had eyes only for my mother now, I was waiting for him to tell me more; she was the next one on the painting.

"Now for the boys; here you have Artur, who lives in Tibet."

"But about my mother?"

"Afterwards Lilly, afterwards. Kneeling down is Armon, he's a sheriff in Romania. He has a strong character, don't rub him up the wrong way. He was the one who discovered that to transform a human was useful for you; it's thanks to him that we, the common vampires, we exist."

"Yes, I know about that, Martin told us about it."

"Very well. Near him, this is Albert."

He sighed on pronouncing my late brother's name. He passed over Alexandre, saying little more than his name.

"And there, that's Agor."

He seemed very proud to present him to me.

"A sage, I like him a lot. Quite often we have great discussions between us both. I've known him as long as Lou: if she hadn't kept me, I would have stayed with him. He lives in Luxembourg, he governs that small country with a rod of iron, but with great wisdom."

Then he became silent, observing us all in turn.

"Which ones do you know personally?"

"I've come across them all during my life. But, I'm closer to some than to others. It's a question of affinities, I suppose."

"How can you remember everything?"

"I'm an Orkani, I'll tell you about what I am. Come, let's sit in the lounge."

Without saying a word, I followed him; at last I was going to find out. We took our places on a red leather sofa.

"We have the duty to remember, this is one of our roles. You'll sometimes see a sheriff accompanied by an Orkani, but this is still rare. In contrast, almost all the members of your family have one. Lou told me everything, or rather she let me see everything in her. My gift of clairvoyance goes beyond what you know of it. I could see the shared moments and they are now engraved in my memory. I am Lou's memory, and therefore also that of all who have been in contact with her at one time or another. I am the witness to their lives, all of their lives. If something terrible were to happen to Lou tomorrow, thanks to me, her memories would survive, and therefore she would still be as powerful even in the afterlife. I'm the guardian of knowledge, the guardian of gifts.

He finished his sentence, closing his eyes, he was above all a sage. I wasn't mistaken; for a few days I'd been thinking of an angel when I've seen him.

He put his hands on me, he wanted to share another very specific point in his life. For him, this technique was a much easier way than with words. I allowed myself to be transported confidently into what he was sharing.

For a brief moment, I saw him lying down, then when the fusion started to work, I found myself in bed within his body. We were now just one.

It was cold, I was shivering. We shivered on this straw mattress underneath just a simple covering. This was a very long time ago, judging by my clothes and the room. This might have been a bedroom, I couldn't be certain, with walls of unadorned stone, and for a window: a simple hole which was barely square.

There was a knock at the door, I noticed that my head was painful. Lou walked into the room looking worried; she came over to my bedside. She placed a damp cloth on my forehead, which was dripping from a fever.

"What have I done wrong?" She thought aloud.

I then realised that this moment was a part of Adrian's transformation into a vampire. He wanted me to know something, something important.

"Excuse me little man," she whispered.

Just as she finished her sentence, she threw herself upon us for one ultimate bite. But it didn't kill us. A strange phenomenon occurred: I floated into the air. Lou was so scared and surprised that she called to her brother.

"Agor, come quickly," she cried out, hysterically.

In less time than it took to say it, he found himself there watching us.

"What's happening to him? What have I done wrong?" She asked.

"Nothing, my sister. You've just saved from death an Orkani," he concluded, smiling and happy at such a discovery.

"An Orkani you say? Mum told us about them. I thought it was a children's story. She never mentioned that they could exist like us."

"An Orkani isn't born until the day of his own death. He can take any form. Had you created one, he would have been different. Keep him with you for eternity, Lorelei. He will be faithful and indebted to you, you have here the best of servants."

Slowly, I felt our bodies cease to levitate, coming to rest gently on the bed. Adrian opened his eyes and saw the world as if he saw it for the first time: with the eyes of a newborn. He started crying because he was hungry.

Hunger for blood, hunger for life and knowledge.

Adrian the Orkani vampire was born.

Slowly, I opened my eyes to see Adrian as he was today.

"She taught you everything while at the same time she was learning from you."

"Exactly Lilly, you've understood it all."

He smiled serenely.

"She treated me like her son, never like a servant. Everything was new to them, as it was for me."

"What was Agor trying to say, when he said that Orkanis could take any form?"

"A vampire killed me, so I became a vampire. If a wolf had killed me, I would have become a wolf."

I remained open-mouthed for a moment on hearing such a declaration.

"What's is the point of having a wolf Orkani?"

"Pack leader perhaps? I admit I don't know."

"Do you know any other Orkani vampires?"

"Of course, I attend many meetings of senior leaders. As some of your brothers and sisters are sheriffs, this permits me to see other Orkanis."

"Yes, you've already told me, I'm stupid sometimes."

He gave me a friendly hug. We had just shared a unique moment. After an instant, he let go of our hug, and I took the opportunity to return to the subject of my mother.

"And my mother?"

"Why am I not surprised?" He said, laughing. "Darren had warned me about your tenacity, this is not just a legend!"

"We are what we are, we never change."

"Indeed."

"So?"

"The unique Lilith! Sent to earth to create a multitude of children among which were ten out of the ordinary... mortals," he began.

"Why did she die?"

"She isn't dead. Who said she'd died?"

"How do you mean?"

"She lives in you, in each one of you."

"We all have a part of our parents in us. In what way is that so exceptional?"

"Before she *"slept"* she asked you, the ten of you, to feed from her."

"You mean to say we ate her?"

I was just stunned by the idea.

"No, no. You fed on her blood. You *"exsanguinated"* her. When her body was nothing more than an empty shell, you put her in a crypt. There, where to this day she still lies asleep."

"Do you mean she could wake up?"

"We could wake her up, but this is not yet the time."

"You will know when it's the time, is that right?"

"No, but you'll know this. It's somewhere deep inside of each of you."

"Where is she, Adrian?"

"I don't know that."

For the first time, he didn't know. He didn't know two important facts. All this left me thinking. Millions of questions poured into all parts of my fully awake brain.

I knew the answers would come in their time, but for the moment this didn't appease me one bit, even in telling myself so.

"And my father, what was his role in all this?"

"He didn't take part in any of your procreations. Fortunately, the poor man never knew about it all. He was just an ordinary human. I'm sorry to tell you."

"So who was my father then?"

"You don't have one."

"You mean to say we arrived thanks to the intercession of the Holy Spirit?"

"Something like that, yes. So as to ensure a balance within nature."

"So we do have our place here then? Legitimately, I mean."

"Yes, like all species on this earth."

All of this was bumping around much too quickly inside my head. I could feel the blood rushing into my temples. I now had to rest.

"That's a lot of information for me Adrian, I think I'll go to relax and unwind a bit, and take it all in."

We'd arrived at the front door; he was about to open it when I put my hand on his arm, interrupting his actions.

"One last question though, please."

"Please, feel free."

"Why are we hiding ourselves?"

"Human Stupidity. Take care of yourself, these two sessions of retrograde viewings must have tired you out. Go straight home, shut yourself indoors, and above all let me know when you've got back."

"I promise, and thanks."

It was easy to find a taxi. The return journey took less long than the trip here: there was less traffic in that direction. I thought about everything I'd learned during the day, but I also enjoyed looking at the scenery. I loved this city.

For no apparent reason, I set myself thinking about Sandrine. I wanted to see her, to talk to her, not of course to entrust my secrets to her, but to have that human contact which I was missing at the moment.

I paid for the taxi, and immediately sent a text message to Adrian to let him know of my safe arrival. The second thing I wanted to do was to eat. I was starving. I got my bottle and sat myself down in front of the television, flipping from channel to channel, sipping the nectar which Darren had left for me.

I fell asleep watching a programme which, I supposed, must have been in Dutch.

Profound Thoughts

Allow me to restore this story into its true reality. Some think that being a vampire is a curse.

My mother's name was Lilith; what comes back to me now is that for her we all were a blessing, a gift from heaven. Ten children, all different certainly, but she loved us just the same, never letting there be any difference between us and our human brothers and sisters.

They, on the other hand, they isolated us because they feared us. Yet during the first twenty years of my life I'd never tasted the blood of a human, instead feeding myself on my Imhumvamp siblings.

The curse; it's humans who created it out of fear.

We're just a different race and humans don't like the difference.

It's human who invented racism and homophobia, not the vampire.

Each race has its mode and manner of survival, it's the way things are. For me, humans have never been just a larder or a blood-bag as some vampires like to call them.

Maybe I'm different.

Maybe our only mistake was to turn a human into a vampire one day, believing this was for our survival.

Because we are different in many ways from what we created. Daylight has never bothered us, we kept our humanity within us; that which our parents bequeathed us.

That goodness so human, as Darren would say.

We are a race of immortals.

If God created us, it's because there's a reason; he never does things by chance, everything has its purpose.

Everything has a place: its place.

When things go out of control due to fear or ignorance, all it brings are lies and fear.

8. News

The ringing of my phone woke me up, I was still on my sofa. The television was displaying merely static. It said five forty-two a.m. on my mobile, it was Darren who was calling me.

"Did I wake you?"

"Hello Darren! Um... yes, I think so."

"How did your day with Adrian go?"

"Very informative. Did you find Alexandre?"

I was speaking to him formally so that he would realise that I knew he wasn't on his own there.

"We are still on the trail, we must prevent him from taking refuge in Germany."

He paused and then continued:

"Lilly, this trip was not yours to do. I had to do it with Lou, and you had to meet Adrian. Do you understand?"

"You mean to say that it was planned?"

"Yes, Lou had planned it this way to accelerate your process of Recouvrance. But also for me, I needed to know who you are. And she is the best placed to tell me about you and all of you. You know; for us simple vampires you are somewhat like legends, unapproachable people."

"Yes, I understand, but promise me again not to change. To neither stop loving me nor to start fearing me."

"I promise. I love you and you know it perfectly; this will not change, whoever you are."

"I love you with all my heart and all my soul Darren, never forget it."

There was a brief silence on the line, I sensed him smiling on the other end.

"What did you learn about Alexandre?" I said.

"Just that he was looking for a way to reach Germany, he wants to join a clan there. A clan which of course would protect him and would endorse his actions."

"He broke the law nevertheless!"

"Yes, that's why we must catch him before he gets there. We're going to a hideout which a reliable informer told us about; at an address in the suburbs of Vienna. Ah! One last thing before I leave you. I warned Martin that Albert had very much been your brother, he's on his way back, so don't be surprised when he arrives. Well, I have to go, we're nearly there. See you soon, remain on your guard."

"Be careful."

Then, he hung up.

The net was closing in around Alexandre. I didn't doubt for one moment that they would return with him.

I put the little blood I had left away in the fridge. I'd almost finished the bottle, more by greed than by need. Then I decided to go about my business despite the early hour.

No sooner had I started, than the phone rang again.

"It's good, we've caught him. We're coming back, we'll be there in the afternoon."

"Ah! Very good," I exclaimed.

"Join us at Lou's place at six o'clock this evening."

I interrupted him.

"How are you feeling?"

"I'm okay, I promise, I'm both relieved and angry. We will have more information tonight. For the time being, he's unconscious. We're coming back, my Lilly, be ready."

"Ready for what?"

"To assist with his interrogation and to discover the truth about all this."

"And if he doesn't tell the truth?"

"Oh, but we have plenty of ways to make him talk! Don't worry about that, but more about the content of what we're going to learn."

"You already know something?"

"Not at all, but I'm expecting the worst. Marie is dead you know, and I have to mourn. So I think that, whatever his motives were, he'll struggle to justify such an act. At least to me," he added, after a moment's hesitation.

"Yes, don't worry, I'll be there to support you and to help you contain your anger too. I love you."

"I love you too," he finished by saying, before hanging   up.

9 The Council

The day was going by at breakneck speed.

It was raining. The aroma emanating from the rain-drenched earth filled me with a certain nostalgia. I loved this aroma, this freshness. It pervaded my mind and my body, giving me some degree of serenity. And that was a good thing, as I was going to need all my composure for Darren and for myself. What's more, I was about to meet other members of my family, and on this occasion, in full awareness of the fact.

The route to the Grand Place was now becoming familiar, even if this time I took the tram. I allowed the city to permeate into me, it was relaxing and pleasant. There were all kinds of people on public transport and I loved that: to feel the essence of a place.

I arrived not far from my eventual destination, I'd have to finish my journey on foot. Even at this slightly later hour, the quarter was still crowded. At a few minutes past six o'clock in the evening, I knocked on the door of Lou's house.

A man who I didn't know, but who I recognised immediately, opened the door. Inwardly, I thanked Adrian. His explanations would save us precious time.

The man held out his hand and introduced himself.

"Hello Lilly, I'm Agor."

"I know who you are."

No sooner had I finished my sentence than he took me in his arms, which surprised me. The simple matter of my telling him that I knew him, had been a green light for him. And what could be more normal than a brother and sister embracing one another.

"It's so good to see you again!"

From simply this contact with his body, memories started to come bursting back inside my head. Our childhood games, our races across the fields, our first hunts together, and my mother's funeral, I could see the crypt where she lies sleeping.

Was this, for us, the means of reminding each other? Did we share everything by simple physical contact?

"Yes, it's very good to see you after so long. I've missed you."

I'd finished my sentence with the realisation that I truly thought that. I smiled at him, he did likewise.

"Come on in. Even if this isn't the best of occasions."

He closed the door and continued:

"Who would believe that one of us would be killed by one of our own!"

"Yes there really must be a reason. Don't forget about Marie also," I added.

He gave me a quick glance.

"I won't forget her."

I held him by the arm, now he looked me in the eye.

"Did you know her?"

"We'd been together for twenty years, and then she met Albert; they fell in love instantly. All I could do was to accept it. So I did know her very well, yes."

"I didn't know that."

"You were there at our wedding; it will come back to you, believe me."

"I don't doubt it for a moment."

I wondered why Marie hadn't recognised me, or perhaps that was another reason for her anger the first few times. She'd known who I was, but couldn't say so. There was apparently a very strict protocol to follow with us, the Imhumvamps. Or maybe she simply hadn't remembered me. I didn't have all the answers, and in this matter I never would.

In any case, something must be occurring while we are in our human phases. It protects us against all forms of danger.

"We have to get on with it, you're the last here. We were waiting for you to start."

I told myself at that moment, that the tram hadn't been the best option. I noted this for next time. I followed him through a maze of corridors; this house was deceptive. Outside, it was small and narrow, and once inside, a veritable labyrinth offered itself before us. The basement must have been spread beneath several buildings, to be so large.

Several minutes passed in silence before he pushed open a heavy wooden door. I immediately felt a dozen eyes fixed upon me. He showed me to my seat, near to Darren. I looked at him out of the corner of my eye; he was clearly alright, but I sensed he was tense and preoccupied. I would have liked to have taken him in my arms, but this wasn't the time for expressions of happy reunions.

They had completed their mission: to bring Alexandre back. Taking my place in silence, I began to let my gaze wander around the meeting.

We were seated solemnly in a circle, sitting on rather strange chairs. They looked more like thrones of old red wood with a high back. They were uncomfortable, I was thankful for the person who'd had the idea to add small cushions to them.

I decided to make a mental roll-call of all those present; until Agor read out the charges laid against Alexandre: the murder of Marie and Albert, which was a reprehensible act according to vampire laws; plus of course his having fled the country.

To my right was Darren, followed by Adrian, who was taking notes. So far, that was simple enough.

Next were my family: Lou and Agor were facing Alexandre. The other side of the circle began with Lizzy, at least I presumed so; next was Martin, who gave me a nod when our eyes met; and Lusiana to finish with, right in front of me. I wasn't sure between Lizzy and Lusiana, they were so much alike. I didn't understand Martin's presence in this place, but the answer would come later as always.

I listened to Agor introducing each of us, which confirmed to me who was who, and he restated the facts. He then addressed Armon, who I couldn't see in the room, which is when I noticed a video screen in front of him and Lou, as well as cameras in the room. We were being watched by one of my absent brothers! Although this room had a rustic feel with its high seats and redwood-covered walls, it was nevertheless very well equipped.

We were in a council chamber, a real one, not improvised like in Darren's club.

Now that the introductions had been done, so to speak, I decided to concentrate on what was going on.

However, my gaze fell upon Alexandre. He seemed much less proud and arrogant here, alone in the centre of the room. I had no memories about him, except those from of the ball, and from the first time I saw him at the chateau.

He was not like us.

He seemed exhausted, his time on the run had drained him without any doubt.

I was astonished at Lusiana's presence here. Adrian had told me that she was close to Alexandre. Darren thought that Alexandre had wanted to join a clan in Germany. I'd certainly wrongly deduced that this had been what he'd wanted to accomplish. Or perhaps Lusiana was here to defend him. An arduous task for the fact that, whatever his reasons, he had broken the law.

History seemed to be repeating itself with this council, but this time it wasn't me who was at the centre of the discussion.

When Agor had finished, a voice resounded in the room. A calm but powerful voice; that of Armon.

"Good evening. Would someone explain to me about Martin's presence here before I continue?"

Agor spoke once again.

"Martin is representing Artur, who can't be here," he explained.

"Very well. Thanks Agor. I'm saddened by what is being played out here tonight. And I'm ashamed, ashamed that within our own family we have a murderer, and that he attacked his own family. Oh, of course it's our destiny to kill, but we strive to do so only in self-defence or to save our lives. This is far from being the case here. Our brother Albert is no more, not to forget about his wife Marie. We are going to try to find out, and in the most courteous manner possible, what motivated Alexandre in such acts.

Armon was speaking as if Alexandre wasn't there.

"And if we fail to understand, if the answers do not bring satisfaction, then each of us knows that we have other means of finding out. For now, let's not descend to the barbarism which Alexandre has lowered himself to.

Now, all eyes were on the accused.

"Alexandre, stand up!" Armon ordered.

With a slow but calculated move, he obeyed. He stared at the floor, his confident presence had vanished with his capture.

"We are listening to you; try to be precise, and you know that no purpose will be served by lying to us."

A little clattering sound behind me caught my attention. I saw a white cat going gracefully through a cat-flap. This was the first time I'd seen an animal in the company of vampires. With his elegant feline footsteps, he skirted along the wall and went to snuggle up on Lou's lap. She began stroking him. I could hear him start purring.

A voice rose up above it:

"I had told them not to touch Marie, this was an accident!"

"Since when do you place your trust in humans?" Darren interrupted.

"They should have obeyed me. They killed her, not me!"

Alexandre was trying to defend himself.

"On your command Alexandre, I'll remind you," Darren insisted, visibly holding back his anger.

Alexandre turned his head towards him.

"You killed them, you've avenged your sister! The rest doesn't concern you."

"And you believe this satisfies me?" Darren shouted, standing up.

"That's enough, you two!" Agor intervened.

Darren took his seat again, clenching his fists.

Then, Armon continued.

"You do yourself realise that you killed our brother? For what reason?"

Alexandre was still standing up, looking at each of us, one by one. Was he looking for some support from one of us?

"This isn't what was planned, I can't stop repeating it to you."

"In that case, tell us then what was intended in the original plan. That which the humans didn't follow," said, very quietly - too quietly even, Lou.

"The plan was that they were to bring Albert to me at the barn."

After a short pause, he added, almost in a whisper:

"Alive."

"You just wanted to see your brother? Why not visit him in that case?" I intervened for the first time.

He gave me a look of contempt and I didn't know why.

"This is all your fault, Lilly!" he said, sharply.

I felt all eyes upon me now.

"My fault? How can it be my responsibility? Only a few days ago, I didn't even know who I really was."

"This was the problem, actually. You came back too soon. He hadn't finished his research. It was therefore necessary to formulate another plan."

I was astonished, I couldn't understand what it was that he was saying, and judging by the silence, I wasn't the only one.

"Who are you talking about?" Armon asked. "What research?"

His voice resounded even more strongly around the room, we were hanging on Alexandre's words, awaiting a response.

"Moonroe," he muttered.

"Speak up," said Armon, exasperated.

"Professor Moonroe."

Now, I was no longer able to get a single sound from my throat. This man in whom I had trusted blindly, and who, I'd thought, had been so good to me during the years of my human phase; that had all been for his own experience.

I'd been a guinea pig! And it was I who'd asked Darren to spare his life. My humanity had been dangerous for us.

At that moment, Martin got up to place himself in front of Alexandre. He put a hand on his shoulder and with a push, forced him to sit down. No one intervened, Martin was well respected.

"What has Professor Moonroe got to do with this story, Alexandre?" He asked, in a very calm tone.

"He wanted the blood of one of us for his research. Since he hadn't had enough time with Lilly, he looked elsewhere."

"Okay. How was he aware of your existence?"

Martin wanted to know everything; I listened attentively.

"That, I do not know," he said, sincerely; anyway it wasn't possible to lie to Martin, who didn't dwell on this response.

"How were you brought into contact with him?"

"Several years ago at a medical seminar."

He looked at us all one after the other, our silence was stressing him, perhaps even so more than the Martin's questions.

"I do love these seminars! They're crammed with easy prey for me," he added with a chuckle. "Moonroe caught me as I was 'drinking' a student. So we, how you might say... got on well."

"You sympathised with him, it's more like you wanted to save your own life by selling your family!" Darren again intervened.

Martin raised his hand to calm Darren, and then resumed.

"Some details I care little about, Alexandre; carry on."

"That man already knew a lot about ourselves: the Imhumvamps and vampires in general. I told him nothing he didn't already know."

Then he looked straight at Darren.

"Yes, I wanted to save my life. He didn't leave me much choice, it must be said. It was either working with him, or death. He is more powerful than you can imagine, and above all he's not alone. His thing in the hospital is just a cover. He's the head of some kind of association."

"What kind of association?" Asked Martin.

"They're working to find a better life for humans. They seek to improve the human gene."

"In what way can vampires help them, in his opinion?" Agor questioned.

"Eternal life says nothing to you brother?" he said sarcastically.

Agor wanted to get up but Lou put her hand on him to calm him down. He immediately sat down with a sigh.

It would be difficult to contain everyone's anger if Alexandre continued in this tone.

"In fact, their ultimate goal is to recreate our gene on a large scale, and then to exterminate us!"

"And you let them do this in total impunity? You didn't consider that when they reached their goal, they would kill you too!" Lizzy asked, speaking for the first time.

"Yes, because they wouldn't succeed! Moonroe trusts me. That's why I stayed with them, to keep an eye on their actions, and in time I would have made you aware of it," he added, rising from his seat.

For the first time, he now felt stronger again.

Alexandre was trying to make us believe that he'd acted like a spy. Being in the situation was certainly a strength, but why hadn't he told anyone? A spy never acts alone, he needs support. I asked myself so many questions. Why did he have Albert killed? Why hadn't the humans followed his orders?

We realised that for Marie it had been an accident. Why had he put his family in danger?

"Why didn't you give your own blood to Moonroe?" I asked.

"I'm just simply a vampire for Moonroe. I didn't interest him beyond that."

"Moonroe didn't ever take a sample of your blood?" I insisted.

"No, as I told you, I didn't interest him."

"How did he know that I was different from other vampires but not you?"

"I don't have all the answers! He must have made a connection between your name and your blood."

"Who among the others does he know about?" Martin resumed.

"He knows only four names: Albert, Laura, Armon and your own," he said, pointing.

An angry murmur rose up among the Council.

"Alright stop," intervened Lou all of a sudden. "Alexandre; tell us all you know even if it means repeating yourself."

"I'd like to know one last thing before he begins, if you'll permit this, Lou?" I asked.

She frowned, but accepted with a nod.

"You let him carry out his studies on me, and yet you knew that I was your sister. Why?"

"Because you had no reason to fear anything. It was just your blood that interested him. He had no reason to kill you as long as he didn't succeed."

"And if he had succeeded?"

"I would have intervened."

"Why should I believe you?"

"Because you're my sister."

"Albert was your brother!" I replied.

"That was an accident."

"Or rather a betrayal by your humans. We have seen how Albert died, filled with silver. His entire body had been filled, there was no chance of coming out of it alive."

"They had disobeyed me, however," he said, by way of finishing.

I motioned to Lou that I was done. She turned back to him.

"We'll listen to you now, don't spare any important details."

We could hear Armon's sigh from the other end of the line. It was hard to take in. For Darren, Martin or me, it was easier, even though it was all barely credible. Martin returned to his seat. Lou now took control.

"I met," Alexandre began, "Professor Moonroe two years ago at a conference about blood which was held in Paris. They pounced on me..."

"Who were they?" Armon asked.

"Moonroe's men; his private security who follow him wherever he goes."

"That organisation; does it have a name?" Armon continued to question.

"Yes, the organisation is called '*Immortalis Sangus*'."

"The message is clear," Martin intervened.

"How can such an organisation be able to be so well established, with a name like that?" Darren wondered aloud.

I agreed with him, it was so big that of course it could hide itself in plain sight.

Lou stood up and asked us to stop intervening if possible, and invited Alexandre to continue. We were having a hard time. So many questions were coming up and we needed answers.

"His henchmen pounced on me while I was discreetly having my dinner in the parking area of the hotel. They brought me to him. He started asking me questions about Imhumvamps. He knew your name." he stated that he'd been watching us. "He wanted to know what I knew about you, etc. I just told him that all of this was just a legend taken from a tale for teenagers."

Alexandre paused and asked for water and something to sustain him. Adrian got up and left the room. We remained silent during the time of his absence which lasted barely more than five minutes. He returned with some water, which he passed to Darren and Martin. As for my family, he gave us a cup full of blood. I was very surprised by the gesture. I looked hard at Darren, trying to get a response, but this came from Lou who came over to me.

"We are all exhausted, we need it. I know this is unusual, but necessary."

She leaned over to me and added:

"We're all family here. Drink!"

She finished her sentence and smiled at me, but she remained standing there in front of me.

I looked at the cup, not with suspicion, but still very surprised at this turn of events, and then raised it to my lips. I tilted the cup and the blood began to flood into my mouth and spread throughout my body. I drank it all in one go! It was wonderfully good. And I had the right to enjoy it.

Lou sat back in her place; she gave me a wink which I reciprocated, smiling at her. She waved her hand toward Alexandre, urging him to continue his story.

"Some time later, he showed me a letter."

He paused deliberately and finished his cup. He insisted on us paying attention, to make himself feel important.

"There were your four names, and brief explanations about vampires, as well as about our family."

Lou intervened.

"Who was this letter from?"

"I don't know, but on the contrary what I do know is that they didn't know enough to be a danger. Those writings made him sufficiently curious to continue and deepen his research, and to expand his association."

"But you helped him to find out more! This is treason," said Martin.

"No; I saved my skin."

He paused once again. Then he continued:

"Alongside your names, there was the notion of your states of being. Beside yours, Lilly, it was noted that you were in a human phase, as well as the name of another doctor."

"What was that name?" I asked.

"A name with an Italian sound to it, I don't know anything more."

"Cabrera," I said aloud.

"Maybe, yes. Something like that."

"What about the others?"

"Their states of being, and their places of residence."

Armon started to shout over the loudspeaker.

"But who could have disclosed such information to him? Who collects such information about us? And why send it all to this guy? There must be a traitor in the entourage of one of us, in fact."

"In what language was this document?" Martin asked, as calmly as ever.

"In Latin," replied Alexandre.

"In Latin? Are you sure?" Martin burst out laughing.

It was rare to hear Martin raise his voice.

"Yes, of course. I know how to recognise Latin. It was a very refined Latin, written in pen and ink."

"Someone has to make sure that Laura is safe."

This sentence had come to be spoken by Lusiana, who was sitting in front of me. She had a very gentle voice. Everyone looked at her now. She hadn't yet taken part in the debate.

"She's right. Either we bring Laura back here, or she must change convent," said Lizzy.

"She won't come here against her will. I'm going to charge myself with the task of Laura's protection and her change of convent. This won't be easy, because she likes it very much there. But I will find a solution," added Lusiana.

My sisters were making their voices heard. They were quieter than the rest of the family, but very protective, perhaps they had also protected me without my knowing.

Adrian noted down each of our words.

"What does it indicate, that the text was in Latin, Martin?" Darren asked.

"This reduces the field of investigation. Who among our entourage is able to speak Latin?"

"I know a little of it," admitted Darren.

"But humans aren't supposed to know about our existence. Apart from Moonroe and his clique, now. So we do indeed have a mole somewhere, foolish and underhand enough to reveal us openly to all. We need to find out who this person is and why they carried out such an act. Moreover, it put him at risk of harm too. This could only be a vampire," concluded Martin.

"Or a wizard," I thought aloud.

I felt all eyes turn to look at me. I looked to Darren for a little support, he immediately understood where I was coming from.

"Lilly's right. The wizards in Scotland knew Albert very well. Since he'd been a wizard before his Recouvrance, and what's more; he had stolen a precious object of theirs..."

"Maybe his death was planned after all!" I intervened. "Say it wasn't an accident, but actually an act of betrayal from Moonroe towards you, Alexandre, because he only wanted his death, and nothing more!"

"But why kill him instead of finding out more about him? Moonroe is primarily a scientist," added Darren.

"Perhaps that was the price Moonroe had to pay in exchange for the wizards' demand for Albert's death. In return, he would get more information about us."

"That rings true," admitted Agor.

Everyone was reflecting on these new and surprising facts, which is when, against all expectations, Alexandre spoke up.

"I'd say it's rather lucky to have encountered this Moonroe, otherwise we wouldn't now be aware of his activities, in my point of view."

"You're right on that point, Alexandre!" Lou cut in, "but you should have let us know straight away!"

I heard a grinding sound, as Alexandre's chair slid backwards and came to rest a few yards away. It was now between Lizzy and myself. We now formed a perfect circle. Any one of our seats could have been in the centre, we were all linked together by rails. In repositioning himself, was he meaning to say that he'd now been forgiven?

Lou stood and sat her cat down on Adrian's lap. We were all staring at her now. She placed herself in front of Alexandre, and asked him to stand up.

No, this was not over yet.

"Not this! No, Lou!" He implored, getting up.

"I have to see everything," she added, simply.

Then she embraced him; one hand on his neck and her other arm beneath his. She immobilised him, I could see terror in Alexandre's eyes. Slowly, she closed her eyes and their bodies lifted off the floor. A strange cry came from Alexandre's mouth while Lou seemed to be singing. The mixture of the two sounds resembled the songs of the sirens, hypnotic and mysterious.

My brother's body set itself trembling, his head lolled back. A blue glow started to emerge from his half-open mouth; she emptied him of his energy. Their entangled bodies began spinning around one-another, and now they seemed to be merging; the more they span around, the more the light dwindled.

Suddenly she left the dance, placing her feet gracefully on the ground a few yards from him. With a gesture of her hand, she pushed him back into his chair without even touching him. His body moulded itself to the shape of the seat, his head leaning to one side; he was unconscious.

As far as I remembered, I had never before seen such a punishment.

She returned to her place in a religious silence. Then she looked right at us, one after the other, before speaking once again.

"He told us the truth. We are in danger, our family and vampires are. We've become prey for Moonroe. Once again, human greed is pursuing us, their thirst for immortality leads them to us again and again. But now, we have more means to fight; there is no question of us vanishing into nature in human form.

She'd drawn off his energy and probed his mind, she knew everything that Alexandre had experienced in recent years. She was now able to develop a plan.

Adrian had said that she was the strongest, he'd omitted to say that she was our leader.

"Lusiana, you're not going to change Laura's convent, you're going to activate her Recouvrance; we need to be complete. Depart right now to Madrid! We'll wait for you back here, in ten days."

The last word had barely been spoken, as Lusiana already left the room.

"Martin, you've been Artur's representative for decades. I'm afraid we'll not be able to convince him to join us. Will you take up this role and combat Moonroe alongside us, as one of us?"

I didn't really understand her question; for me Martin was one of us even though he wasn't my brother.

He stood up and prostrated himself before my sister. This situation was becoming more and more bizarre to me.

She said nothing and turned towards Darren.

"Darren, come here please," she invited him, with a wave of her hand.

They were both at her feet, and me; I was lost. I lacked the knowledge to understand what was being played out here and now. I was just a spectator, but Darren was mine and I was worried.

She placed a hand on each of them. I started to get up in protest when a voice came ringing into my head.

"Leave her be. She will do them no harm; she's officially welcoming them into the family, this way they will have all the powers too, Lilly."

I immediately recognized the wise sound of Adrian's voice, I looked at him; he smiled at me. Slowly, I sat back in my place.

"Okay. Thanks."

A heavy silence reigned, for me. I could see Martin's and Darren's eyelids fluttering rapidly. What was she doing to them? I could no longer remain in ignorance.

"Adrian, what's she doing?"

"She's initiating them. She's providing them with some knowledge and giving them some gifts."

"Gifts?"

"Yes, for example rare gifts they might need in the battle in which we're about to engage."

"She can do that?"

"She can do all; give all and take all away again too."

"Why has she inherited so much ability?"

"You all have, Lilly. It's just that she's been appointed to be your queen, but she detests that word, so she doesn't assert her title all over the place. You understand?"

"She's humble. Yes I understand. Our mother chose her?"

"Yes, it was your mother who made that choice. Lou was the first-born, it was legitimate. And as I've told you: she is the strongest among you all."

"I very much believe you."

After a few minutes, which seemed like an eternity, she took her hands away again, and addressed herself to Adrian.

"Give me the cups, please."

Adrian gave them to her. I watched her, curious about what was to follow. She bit her wrist, allowing her royal blood to fill them. Then she offered them around.

"Drink every last drop."

While they were complying, she placed her hands on their heads and began to mumble. This lasted for only a few seconds. Then, she invited them to take their places again.

She turned next, to Lizzy; she was dispensing her orders one after the other.

"Lizzy, I want you to go over and pay a visit to these wizards in Scotland. I want to know everything; their motivation and their intention. Their chief is called Polvus and they live in a village called..."

"Stonehaven, Lou; I've been there before, in order to visit Albert."

"Ah! very good. Do you know the wizard?"

"No, but I'll find him easily, don't worry."

"Once you have the information, tell it to me. But stay there, watching their every move. You're our eyes and ears in Scotland."

As with Lusiana, Lizzy went on her way immediately. Funny this family who say only a brief hello, and not goodbye.

She turned around with a smile towards Agor.

"You, you stay here with me."

Without saying a word, she turned back to Adrian and rested her hand on his arm. He closed his eyes by way of acquiescence. My turn came next; what was she going to ask of me?

"Lilly. We could say that you've chosen the moment well for entering your Recouvrance," she said with a laugh. "But we have no choice. I do know that many things must seem strange to you."

"This is true indeed."

"But you're well looked after. You have strength, knowledge and wisdom from Martin. Darren is still young and impetuous, but his future within our family will bring him what he's missing."

She really was speaking like a Queen.

"You'll go back to France and in your luggage you'll bring Alexandre."

I was going to intervene, when she raised her hand.

"Alexandre will be our spy within "*Immortalis Sangus*." He will continue what he started, but this time under our supervision. To be more exact, that of yours. He will live with you, be accountable to you, and with the slightest '*faux pas*'..."

She cast a glance towards Alexandre, we all turned our head to him.

"There will be none, sister!" said Alexandre, who had just regained consciousness.

"There will be no '*faux pas*'... Very well, Alexandre. I'll let you develop your plan. Back here in ten days' time, or even sooner, I want complete information and if needs be I'll organise a new council. I wish you all a safe journey back."

"Armon doesn't have a task?" I asked.

I wanted to know what each of us would be doing, I was fed up of being in the dark; so from that moment on, I wanted to know everything.

"Armon, yes! I'd almost forgotten you. Thank you, Lilly!"

Now she spoke into her monitor.

"Watch over her, Armon."

She enounced this phrase with great gentleness. You could detect the love and tenderness there.

"Watch over who?" I inquired softly.

"Our mother, Lilith."

She walked over to me and offered me her embrace. I stood up, slightly worriedly, and nestled against her.

We were running in a field full of poppies, the weather was lovely. We were young, still children. Our yellow aprons twirled all around us; the more we ran, the more we laughed aloud. In the distance, there was a woman sitting in the grass. As we came over to her, we stopped ourselves dead. She looked up at us and started to smile.

"My little girls, come closer so I can present to you your little brother."

She stared at him with love.

"He is like you, he received the gift. What do you think of the name Armon?"

"Yes Mummy, it's very beautiful. He will always protect you, I sense it," said Lorelei to our mother.

"You're my little queen, Lorelei," she said, softly stroking her cheek.

I went over to her, at least the little Lilly of that time did.

"And me, Mother?"

"You, you're my princess, I love you so much, you look so fragile and yet so strong," she said, kissing my forehead.

"I prefer princesses, they're nicer," I said, chuckling.

"A queen needs her princess to help keep her head on her shoulders and remain modest. You'll know to do that I think, Lilly?"

"I promise it, Mother."

"Where is Lusiana?" she asked me.

"She didn't want to run with us, so she stayed at home with our father," I replied.

"Very good, go quickly and join her."

She finished her sentence with a smile, then she gave me a pat on the bottom.

Lou let go of me for a moment and then resumed her embrace. This time we were adults and all were present. There was snow here, my brothers were carrying a coffin upon their shoulders, my sisters and I were walking behind them. Artur led the way alone.

The cold didn't seem to affect us while we followed a path through the forest, we were more preoccupied with the purpose of our walk. Artur cut away some branches, which cleared our way towards a clearing. The reflection of the sun on the snow conveyed something magical to both the location and the moment.

Artur motioned for us to stop. He knelt down and pushed away the snow with the back of his hand, this same snow was obstructing a plaque on the ground. He pulled on the ring, and this unveiled to us a staircase of stone; we followed it into the bowels of the earth, to reach a room lit by torches. In the middle of this, a catafalque awaited my mother's coffin. No other tombs were discernible here. They placed her gently there, and all in a circle now, kneeling down, we bid our temporary farewells to our mother.

Like Sleeping Beauty, she would await the moment of her revival.

Lou took a step back, smiling at me; these moments of Recouvrance offered by my brothers and sisters were helping me to recover my memory. We were bound together much more than we could think or believe. When one of us disappeared, it was a part of our history that vanished forever. The more I learned, the more I hated Alexandre for what he'd done to our family. I still couldn't understand why.

"Thanks," was once again the only word that came to me.

"Go now, we must hurry ourselves and get this situation under control. This is neither the first nor the last time we'll fight, only this time we have a trump card! We're in the know, and it falls to us to reap the benefit of victory," Lou concluded.

As I was leaving the room, I took one last glance at Adrian. He still had much to teach me. I could see in his eyes that he supported me, that he was there for me. It would suffice that I didn't forget this detail.

Arriving outside, the crowd intoxicated me. I hadn't expected so many people and particularly not that it would now be daytime.

How many hours had we remained cloistered in? Darren brought me out of my daydreaming, by taking my hand.

"Come Lilly, the car is parked a little further away. We must hurry up."

"Aren't you tired from your journey?" I asked. "From that night? From all those emotions?"

He came up close to me and submerged his gaze into mine.

"I'm doing fine thanks, and you?"

"Let's say that I'm trying to sort things out and understand it all."

"You'll have time on the way back to rest and reflect. At the chateau we'll take a little time for ourselves," he said, finally.

"I'd love to."

He kissed me on my lips. Straight afterwards, we took to the road with Martin and Alexandre: in the direction   of   France.

Recouvrance

This transition between my two conditions was pleasant. Still in my last human life, I immersed myself, step by step, back into my real life.

For the moment, I had no idea why I had this need to flee from the vampires.

Adrian had spoken of Paris in the eighties. What had happened to me in Paris which had so badly wounded me to the point of my having the urge or the need to escape?

For now, I knew very little of this, certainly very rich and long, period in the past. I was hoping that everything would come back into my memory with neither disappointment nor regret.

Nobody would evoke the deeds of the past, or seldom if so, out of respect; either because this was the rule, or without doubt out of modesty, leaving us to choose for ourselves what was good to know.

But one thing was certain: when we were human, there was nothing in our knowledge or our vampiric experiences which did not return to the surface.

There was nothing we presupposed about who we were, right up until our bodies or our souls wanted to return to our truth.

So, the Recouvrance began.

A phase where maybe lots of things were permitted. But above all, that of the hope for something better.

Our lives were just an eternal new beginning, eventually leading to perfection, if that was possible.

10. The Way Back

The journey went quickly and quietly, as Darren had predicted. We were all physically and emotionally exhausted. I suspected Martin had already worked out a plan of attack.

Darren's attention was on the sky and Alexandre was sleeping. I couldn't make my brother out at all. I was very suspicious about him. I don't think I'd ever loved him. He looked so different from us, so little involved in our family, so little concerned about our safety. He was selfish. But why was he like that? Why did he act in that way?

For the time being, I was hoping that Darren could overcome his anger. Once this story was over, I'd let him do whatever he wanted with Alexandre, who still remained, indirectly, Marie's killer.

Alexandre was under the responsibility of Martin, which, in my opinion, wasn't a bad idea. However, they decided that they would both be staying with us.

On our arrival at the chateau, I hurried back to my room. I needed to get changed and to get my bearings again. Darren intercepted me in the hallway.

"Where are you running to like that, Lilly?"

"To my room!" I replied, surprised by his question.

He pulled me close to him, smiling.

"We could share a bedroom together. You could come into the part of the house that's strictly for me."

He was trying to arouse my curiosity, but I would have come along even without this last detail.

I turned around slightly, pointing to the door of my room.

"Shall I just get my things?"

"You won't need anything, believe me."

He finished his sentence by taking my hand. We took the opposite route from my room, entering the library.

"It's in the wing which you don't yet know."

With these words, he pressed a button under his desk, which opened an undetectable door to the left of the window.

A red-carpeted corridor opened onto a small vestibule presenting three doors. Always three doors, which was a strange feature. This chateau was truly a labyrinth.

"We've taken a shortcut. I'll have to give you a tour of the entire house, which is now yours. But another day. Come!"

I followed him without saying a word. Anyway, I was now lost. He opened a door for me.

"If Madam would care to enter," he said, taking a bow.

I smiled at him, shrugged my shoulders back in return, and religiously placed a foot inside his lair.

"So here's my bedroom, no; our room," he corrected himself.

Next, he opened another door: the bathroom!

Dumbfounded, I observed this place, which he'd been able to hide from me up until now. He was very proud of it. I ventured into the bathroom.

It was tiled, and blue from floor to ceiling, but the lower part was sea-blue and the rest sky-blue. This gave a depth and a strange sense of being able to drown here. Next, there was the shower; I'd never seen such a large one, with a little bench for two inside, somewhat like in saunas. It was located in the middle of the far wall; it was more rectangular than square and was surrounded by a wall of transparent glass. There was no sink or bath, just this gigantic shower area and a few cupboards.

"Would you like to take a shower?" He asked.

Who would want to miss out on this?

"I wouldn't say no. I feel myself to be dirty from the journey and all those recent events. I need to wash it all away."

He stood behind me; softly, he rested his hands on my hips and gave me a hug. I closed my eyes and felt his fingers unbutton my blouse. I had neither the strength nor the will to struggle. I let him brush against my skin; each of his actions, each of his caresses awakening my passion for him. I was naked now; he gently pushed me to the shower and undressed while still holding me. Our skins were still touching.

He came in with me and started the water running. I felt it trickling over me; Darren now accompanied this with his soft hands in order to cover me all over in that redeeming moisture. I felt his hands following the contours of my curves, finishing on my bottom. He applied a slight pressure, which had the effect of making me open my eyes. I smiled at him when I realised that he was still mostly dry, since the water had barely reached him yet. As I'd wanted to share this moment and this feeling with him; with a quick, precise movement, I swapped places with him. It was his turn to be pampered.

In the same way as he'd done, I spread the water all over his body with caresses which were full of tenderness. This little game lasted a few minutes, during which he didn't close his eyes. He also wanted to enjoy the sight before him.

"Are you ready?" He said to me.

"Ready for what?" I asked, surprised.

"To receive the rain..."

I frowned.

He operated a button which I hadn't noticed before on the wall, and a light rain began to fall in the shower area. The water came from above our heads; he turned the handle to speed up the flow.

I looked up above; seeing the droplets falling over me as if in slow motion, I was overcome by laughter. It was an insane sensation. That freshness permeated my mind, cleansing me all the while.

We were laughing ourselves to death when he came closer to me and embraced me. I was full of joy.

"I'm happy to be back at the chateau, and that you're here beside me," he whispered.

"Me too. We should ask for a little time for ourselves you know; for us, and for me to finally get things off my chest."

"Speaking of which, I took the opportunity of bringing your clothes here."

"You did well! Thanks very much."

"You should give up your home, Lilly; save on the rent and all the rest. And your cats are very well used to being here now, in case you're asking yourself the question."

"Oh! I'll forget my head one day too; I hadn't even remembered that they were here. Thanks Darren, you're a love," I said, giving him a kiss.

Our kiss lasted for several minutes. He turned off the water, lifted me up and laid me gently on the bed. Unlike our first night in Belgium, where our desire for one another was finally able to fully express itself after many months of temptation, this night had been more tender.

Not that our passion had already dwindled, but because we needed tenderness and gentle gestures. This passion had many faces and up until now, they all suited me. The different facets of Darren filled me with more joy than I could ever have hoped for.

I loved him without concession.

I rested my head on his shoulder, relaxed and serenely. My eyes began to explore this room, our room.

It was twice as big as mine and its unique feature was its roundness in the part facing the outside. We were within one of the towers of the chateau, probably the one on the left. In the rounded area was a large bay window.

On the other hand, the curtains were burgundy like my ones. The bed meanwhile wasn't a four-poster, but more recent and very large; easily more than two yards wide. I was lost in it, this wasn't a feeling, but a fact.

I was lost in it as I was lost in Darren.

Dawn awoke me; I set a foot down and walked over to the bay window. The garden was still covered in fog. This view reminded me of my first days here, of my marvel at seeing such a scene.

Now, things had changed, but certainly not the sense of security and tranquillity that this chateau brought me. This sensation had been strengthened by everything that had come to pass, everything I'd learned about myself. I had nothing to fear here with Darren. He was right, I should bring back the rest of my belongings and make this place my home.

I saw in the distance, the door of Hector's home open and their dog running off down the lane which led to the road outside. A hissing sound rang out, which stopped him in his tracks, immediately making him turn around.

Hector had positioned himself on the doorstep, a cat in his arms. I recognised Tenshi, my Turkish cat. With his white and ginger coat, he was clearly visible against Hector's black outfit. He'd also left his fur on it. He seemed serene in the company of a vampire. I wondered whether Darren would allow cats to come inside the house.

"Yes, they can come into the ground floor; anyway they follow Hector everywhere..."

I slowly turned around to him. He got up to join me in admiring the scenery.

I nestled myself in his arms and said one thing only:
"Thanks".
"For?"
"For the cats," I said, softly.

Then, with a wave of my hand, I pointed out the gardens.

"For all of this. And also, for being you."

This   day   promised   to   be   fine.

11. The Plan

It was nine o'clock in the morning, and a good time to emerge from our cozy cocoon.

To get to the kitchen, Darren showed me the normal route which was, admittedly, a little longer than the one we used the previous day. But that was no matter, soon this place would hold no more secrets for me!

As was usual for him, Hector was busying himself around the coffee machine. The chateau dictated the course of his daily life. Martin was there having a conversation with Alexandre.

No sooner was I back in the kitchen than my cats came running over to me; they recognised me! I crouched down to take them in turns in my arms and to give them cuddles. They had missed me!

It wasn't until afterwards that I said hello to the others.

I particularly went over to see Hector, while Darren went to sit over with Martin and Alexandre around the island unit.

"Good morning Hector, I'd like to thank you for how you're looking after my cats: I saw you this morning, they seem to love you!"

"Good morning Miss Lilly, it's good to see you here again. It's a pleasure to take care of your little animals," he replied, a little embarrassed.

He certainly wasn't used to being complimented. I placed my hand on his shoulder as a sign of friendship.

I greeted the others and sat myself down by my cup. For the time being, I would just listen.

Alexandre would continue to be what he had been, a spy. But he was ordered to return here every evening, and above all to give us a report on the developments in the situation.

Martin suggested that Philip should make the acquaintance of Moonroe, since he himself had been "*exposed*" to his view. In order to do this, Darren was responsible for getting back in contact to arrange another interview; this would seem consistent.

Alexandre told us that the next conference was being held in a week's time, which would be a good opportunity for Darren to don his journalist's costume. During the interview, he would introduce Philip to Moonroe, if the opportunity arose. On the other hand, we needed to know above all, what were the official motives of the '*Immortalis Sangus*' association. We knew that the conferences had as a major theme that of the blood, but what else was there to find out about? What could be the benefit which Philip could offer, to make him indispensable in the eyes of Moonroe, within his organisation?

We had to smuggle ourselves in there for several reasons: to keep an eye on Alexandre, but also to gain a different, and scientific, perspective of the actual situation. And of course, in order to watch over Moonroe without respite.

Martin and I wouldn't be able to do anything with him directly. He knew us for what we were. Our roles would have to take place in the shadows. In contrast, for him Darren was a journalist; the fact of having already interviewed him would facilitate this second contact and the making of an appointment. We had the advantage.

While they continued to construct the plan, I began my own research on the internet.

The association had been founded by Professor Moonroe a few years ago. To date, it had over four hundred members, which scared me a little. Were these four hundred people vampire hunters? Their primary purpose was to carry out research on blood enzymes. A memory came back into my mind, of an observation which Moonroe had made to me once about the composition of my blood and this enzyme which he hadn't known about. Things started to become clearer; in hindsight he hadn't been very careful! Of course, their website didn't mention that they were doing research on vampires in order to acquire eternal life... And this was no bad thing. We didn't need any more of this kind of publicity.

I closed my laptop.

"Well, Lilly?" Asked Darren

"Nothing much, apart from what we'd already known," I began, addressing myself to them. "The association has four hundred members and their research focuses on blood and its composition. Nothing more than that. Moonroe seeks the enzyme, he had spoken about it with Darren during the interview. Do you remember?"

"Yes, very well. I already have a good reason to approach him again."

At that instant, a strange phenomenon occurred. A thick smoke filled the room, the cats ran away very indignantly into the garden. Everyone got up, ready to attack but above all, very much out of surprise. One shouldn't be so easily able to enter Darren's home; his security system had let him down.

From out of the smoke, there came a voice.

"Good morning, Lilly."

I immediately recognised the voice of Adrian. It was a relief, but what was this phenomenon; some sort of magic?

"Uh! Good morning Adrian. What..."

"Sorry for the sensational entrance." He dusted himself off while he was speaking. "Just a moment please."

The scene was now rather amusing. I had an impression of déjà vu, but from where? A fraction of a second later, Lou appeared. My eyes widened more and more. How had they done that?

"Good morning everyone," she said.

A communal hello echoed throughout the room, while we were waiting for further explanations. Suddenly, Martin started to laugh. Comical character.

"So this power is real, Adrian?" Said Martin.

"Oh yes," he answered, simply. "The power of the Orkanis is immense."

He said that while looking at me. I frowned.

"Dematerialisation, Lilly. In essence, I have the power to transport myself and to bring along with me who I want, wherever I want. However, it's to be used sparingly."

"Seriously?" I exclaimed.

I was speechless.

"Yes, seriously."

He stepped back to make room for Lou, who had now put her hair back into place, this action not being without aesthetic consequence.

"I'm the bearer of rather disturbing news. Lusiana has disappeared, we don't have any news of her. She was in

Madrid with Laura as planned, for her Recouvrance, which was going slowly but normally. We now have several problems. First, we need to know where Lusiana is, and secondly find Laura as soon as we can, since she's alone now, before she does something stupid. We've been through a similar case before, and the result is not the best!" She said, by way of finishing, looking hard at Alexandre.

I didn't really understand this last insinuation aimed towards Alexandre; this which explained what? His indifference, his heartlessness? This excused him just a little? The more I observed him, the more I tried, unsuccessfully, to soften myself towards him.

"So I'll apologise in advance, but I'm probably going to have to thwart your plans," she said, with a sigh.

She paused for a time, staring hard at us, one after the other. Whatever her plan was, we had very little to say in any case. Just to follow her orders for the sake of our family, our vampire race, and probably the humans too.

"Lilly, you're going to go with Adrian to Madrid. Over there, a lookout man gave us some indications that may well relate to Laura, even if they're not yet confirmed."

"Okay, anyway I'm not very useful here at the moment."

I looked at Darren.

"We have no choice, I'm sorry."

"I know, Lilly, and you're quite right, you can't do anything with Moonroe. Look after your sister, she has more need of it."

"But we'd been apart and yet here I am going again!"

"I know..."

"I'll go and get some things ready," I said, leaving the room.

On the staircase, I heard Darren telling Adrian once again to take great care of me.

My Recouvrance was going well, but I would have liked a little respite to spend more time with Darren, just him and me. So I could finally get to know him better, and especially to better find out who I was.

I threw the essentials into my bag, I didn't know how long I was going to be away, but this time I brought with me enough to last for more than a weekend! One last look at this room, which I wanted to keep in my memory, and then I went back downstairs to join the others. Midway down, Darren joined me.

"What's going on?" I asked, surprised to see him.

He came over to me in silence. He took my bag from my hand and placed it on the floor to give me a hug.

"Nothing, I wanted to say goodbye to you away from the others," he said softly, smiling at me.

I felt his sadness, in view of this new separation.

"Is your own life always so hectic, Darren?"

"Yes, almost. But until now I'd been alone and it didn't matter about all that traveling and the other meetings. Now with you, everything is different."

I didn't let him finish.

"At the moment, it's my family which has come to disrupt your life."

"Your family doesn't bother me. I understood once Lou had told me what you were; I understood what was at stake and the aims. In that way, I accepted the sacrifices which that would demand."

"You certainly know more about it than I do up to now. Yes, the stakes are high; I feel it deeply within my being. Like I feel you here too now; you are within me Darren. I'm bringing you with me, the distance and time won't change this feeling.

He tenderly touched his lips to mine. Gently, I bit him and drank his blood, he did likewise. Our fluids blended together and circulated through our veins; we were as one.

"That's all I wanted to hear, Lilly."

"For eternity, Darren."

On those words, I picked up my bag and rushed down the stairs, I didn't want him to see my tears. I made one stop before the kitchen in order to pull myself together.

"Are you ready, Lilly?" Lou asked me.

"Yes, I am," I said, on the doorstep.

I turned my head one last time, just as I was entering the room to join Adrian, but Darren didn't appear.

I positioned myself near to Adrian, not knowing what to do, smiling at everyone as if I was at ease and had the situation under control.

"Bon voyage and good luck to you both," said Lou.

"Thanks, and see you soon I hope," I answered, grimacing and looking at Adrian.

"Alright, Lilly; give me your hand and let yourself go," he said, calmly.

"I hardly have the choice."

He took my hand, and the instant afterwards, I was there: in a square.

An ordinary square which was dotted around with trees and benches. I felt a little dazed. I felt a pressure on my right arm. I turned my head and Adrian appeared like magic. My first reaction was to look all around us, but life was just carrying on here. After all what could be more normal than seeing two people appear from out of nowhere, and land in a square in the mid-morning! The sun was facing me, it burned me. I would hate Spain.

"So how was it?" Adrian asked excitedly.

"Quick," I replied.

"That's it?"

"Well, yes, did I miss something?"

"No, you must be one of those people for whom teleportation has no effect. What a shame; it's quite funny sometimes," he said, a little disappointedly.

"Funny how?"

"Well, some people vomit, others simply have nausea."

"And you find that funny! Adrian, you are a child!" I exclaimed.

"Most probably you're right. Too bad."

He looked all around.

"We should avoid being in direct sunlight. Ah! I hate the countries in the South. Come on," he said, finally.

"Where are we going?"

"Into the shade, so I can think."

I followed him underneath a large tree.

"What's the plan, Adrian?"

"We need to find the lookout man, then make sure he's got something good to say about Laura. Next, we have to find her and bring her back."

"And Lusiana?"

"Later, one thing at a time. Look!"

He pointed towards a house.

"This is the where the lookout man lives. Come and see him."

"Is he expecting us?"

"He won't be surprised at our visit."

"Is he a vampire?"

"Yes, he's a vampire."

He said this with an air of amusement.

"You shouldn't mock me, Adrian."

He stopped still and turned towards me, looking very serious this time.

"I'm not mocking you, on the contrary, your innocence enchants me. Such freshness, Lilly! I've spent centuries in the company of vampires; old ones, very old. This is the first time I've seen an immortal during a phase of Recouvrance so close up, and I confess that I find it very refreshing."

He thought for a moment and reiterated:

"Yes, very refreshing. So, the idea of mocking you is far from my mind."

Then, he continued on his way to the lookout man's white house. I stayed there watching him walk away.

"Are you coming, Lilly?"

"Yes of course, forgive me."

My thoughts were confused, it must have been the effect of the teleportation, but it gave me no pleasure to tell him about it.

He knocked on the door.

A woman opened it. Without a word, she turned around and shouted.

"Diego, it's for you!"

Without even a hello, she left again. I looked at Adrian.

"Charming Spanish hospitality!"

A second later, a man came to the door. He was tall, over six feet, and imposing. He stared hard at us from head to toe; to me this moment seemed not to end, when finally he spoke to us.

"Good morning, please excuse my wife. You've come for the intruder, I presume."

"Good morning Diego. Yes, we've come for her. I'd like to introduce Lilly to you; I'm Adrian."

He shook our hands in turn. I gave him barely audible hello. He closed the door again and invited us to follow him beneath a pergola a little further into his garden, in the shade.

"She arrived two days ago. I noticed her because she frightened my wife's children. It seems to me that this is a young vampire, she doesn't seem to be in the best condition. Nevertheless, she goes out at night and that's dangerous for her and for us. Look for yourselves."

He handed us a newspaper clipping describing a mysterious death. The article mentioned that it was probably an animal attack.

"Why didn't you help her?" I asked.

"It's not my role, her progenitor should have done that, but apparently he took off!"

"You've never seen her accompanied by a young woman?" Adrian asked.

"No, never."

"Where does she live?" He continued.

"In the church! Surprisingly: I don't know how the priest can harbour her without sensing a difference in her. And I don't know why she's spared him."

I looked over at the modest red building. I told myself that it was almost logical that Laura should find refuge in a church, after spending several years in a convent. It was her only point of reference for the moment, without Lusiana or anyone to help her and guide her during her Recouvrance.

"Okay, is there anything else we should know?" Adrian asked, standing up.

"No, not to my knowledge," said Diego, offering us his hand.

"Thanks Diego," I said.

"You're welcome Madam, I'm just doing my job."

Adrian, in turn, took his leave of him, and then we headed off to the church.

"That was quick."

"Yes, it wasn't necessary to prolong this. What's more, I don't like those vampires married to humans."

"Why not?"

"It is dangerous for us all. That's all."

"Me, I find it good. This proves that humans can be tolerant and that vampires know how to cohabit without taking a bite out of everything lying around. This gives hope for the future."

"Once you have recovered your entire memory, maybe you'll change your mind," he said, sadly.

"What do you mean?" I asked, holding him by the arm.

"That there are very few examples which conform to your expectations, I'm sorry."

"What are you talking about?"

He took a step toward me and put his finger to my mouth. Very tenderly, he told me:

"This is neither the time nor the place. All in good time; things will come back to you soon enough. Don't forget that if you had to become human, there's a reason for that. Sometimes it's also an escape, not just for your own protection... uniquely... from humans."

"What if I don't remember? You'll help me to find out?"

He stayed there silent before me.

"I don't know," he said, in all true sincerity.

With these words, as he pushed open the heavy door of the church, the coolness lashed our faces and it made us feel good. I didn't press the point for the moment.

A strong smell of incense filled my nostrils as we walked down the aisle. Was this smell there to hide other ones? A man was kneeling before the altar. Judging by his attire, he ought to be the master of this place. He slowly stood up and made a sign of a cross before turning towards us. Then he came over to meet us, his hands folded on his stomach.

I felt no hostility emanating from him. He approached us without fear. He smiled while he spoke to us.

"Good morning, what brings you into the house of God?"

"Good morning, Father," Adrian replied. "We're looking for a young woman. We were told she'd found refuge with you."

"Do you have a photo of this young woman?" He asked.

We weren't expecting such a question.

"She's my sister. She's has ginger, shoulder-length hair with green eyes. Her name is Laura."

"Ah! Yes, Laura," he said, pensively.

The clergyman seemed to believe me and trust us, his period of reflection confirmed at least one thing: he knew her.

"She's a bit lost and her reasoning is lacking."

He rolled his eyes and offered his hands towards the sky.

"But God knows how to bring her back to us. He will show her the path to follow."

"Is she still with you?"

He stared at me, but my look made him lower his eyes.

"Yes, she's still here. Come; I'll show you where she lives."

To the right of the altar, there was a small wooden door, which we passed through to find ourselves in a small cloister. We followed the priest, and I admired the roses that grew all along the stone columns. A pretty fountain, overlooked by a dove, took pride of place at the centre. Four paths led to it.

Arriving at a door, the priest stopped and knocked.

"Laura! You have visitors," he said.

He threw us a glance, smiling.

"Laura?" He asked, insistently.

After a few seconds, he turned to us apologetically.

"I think she's not here," he said, finally.

"Could we go and wait inside?" Adrian asked.

"I don't know if she would allow that," he added, blocking our way.

Adrian put his hand on his shoulder and looked him in the eyes, suggesting to him:

"We can wait inside. She will be happy about our visit. You can trust us, Father."

Then, he removed his hand, the priest tottered a little; I even thought he might fall.

"Alright, do as you please. I should return to my prayers."

"Thanks, Father," said Adrian.

"Thank you," I said.

Then, he left to go back to his presbytery.

"What did you do to him?"

"A small suggestion that he'd accept. He won't come back to see us, so we can be left in peace to seek and find whatever we need."

Gently, Adrian pushed the door open in front of us, offering an austere room before us. There was nothing on the walls except for a crucifix. The furnishings were basic: a simple wooden bed, a bedside table with a drawer, made from the same dark wood. Facing the bed was a small odd desk, and between these two there was a single-paned window letting a little light in. This place was ideal for meditation.

The room called for silence, for peace and quiet; for my sister maybe repentance. I sat down at the desk, while Adrian rifled through a small chest of drawers beside the entrance door. Some scribbled-on papers were scattered on the desk, the little I could decipher seemed confused and disorganised. Lou had been right, I was starting to understand the necessity of being accompanied during the Recouvrance. This little renaissance was delicate in many ways. My knee bumped into a small drawer under the desk. I hadn't seen it until just then. I bent down and managed to open it. Inside there was a bible: I flipped through it, it was all crossed out in red. A notebook and pen accompanied the holy book; the pen wasn't red, I like to think it was the previous tenant who had mistreated the bible. That which I knew of my sister, was that she was pious; coming to take refuge here was fine evidence of it.

I took the notebook out, and looked through it. It was Laura's diary. I didn't dare to read her lines. Would it reveal her privacy? Her deepest thoughts? Her disarray or her fear perhaps. For the moment, I had no memory of this sister.

"Did you find anything?" Adrian asked, breaking the silence.

"Laura's diary," I replied, looking up at him.

He sat down beside me; the diary seemed to be the only thing of interest in this room for the time being, since my sister wasn't here. I saw him bend his head over and bury his hand into the drawer. He pulled out a simple ring, but in gold. He turned it around in every direction in order to look for any clue about it.

"Is it Laura's?"

"Yes, her name's engraved on the inside," he said, pointing to the tiny engraving which had been done on the ring.

"Why did she take it off?"

"The diary will perhaps tell us," he said.

"Do you think we should read it? Doesn't it bother you to invade her privacy?"

"We need to, Lilly; we have to find her. You understand?"

"Yes, of course I understand."

I opened the notebook at the first page and began to read.

12. Laura's Diary

If you are reading these words, it's because I'm dead... or worse still. I have been unmasked.

Tuesday

Lusiana has disappeared, I don't know what to do. I sought asylum in a church. God is my refuge. I've found a part of myself again. The world today is not what it was, far from it. Very violent and scattered all around with souls in distress. Writing for me is still a comfort.

I'm trying to curb my thirst. I tried to leave one man alive, but seeing his suffering, I had to finish him off. Where are you Lusiana? You said you were my sister!

There are children here, they shout too loudly, my head will explode. I went to see them, I wanted them to stop. I hurriedly took myself outside, they were there playing with the leaves. I also felt the wind lash my face. The sky is grey, this doesn't bode well. The wind drives the clouds along at a dizzying speed. So I went over to them, those who were still playing in the leaves... Then one of them yelled out, pointing at me. The child began to cry her eyes out, so I cast a quick glance towards the house and saw the parents running over. The father approached me, he spoke to me but I didn't understand anything he was saying, then he leaned forwards to me without fear and whispered: "You're scaring the children, go back home, go and feed yourself, you need it... But don't touch them!" Who is this man? What's happening to me? I came here to pray, but no one's responding to me. However, God spoke to me. He gave me a mission; to cleanse this city of its crooks and lost souls. There's a bird outside that accompanies me. His song soothes me. The street lights are lit at last. I'm thirsty, I'm torn by it, I don't believe that Lusiana is going to come back again, and the priest can't help me. I have to get out of here!

I raised my head up towards Adrian.

"She's not well, she's rambling. We must find her. This must be horrible. Was it Diego that she met?"

"Yes, probably, at least I hope so. Carry on, Lilly."

I dived back into her writings, which had touched me; I felt her fear, her loneliness. How horrible to endure all of this!

"No!" I said, suddenly. "Try a faster way to locate her and find out what she's been doing!"

"Okay," replied Adrian, understanding the urgency of the situation.

He put the ring in the middle of the notebook, took hold of my hand, and together we left to join Laura, in the near and still fresh, past.

She appeared, we saw her, but we knew we couldn't intervene; the past was the past. Once more, I was confronted with a reality which was certainly going to displease me. It was imperative to find her, and for this we would need to know what she'd been doing. Where could she be? What better than her writings and the visions of her world to guide us!

It was night-time, she was pacing up and down the streets of old Madrid. These quarters were not suitable places for a girl on her own, we had cause to fear the worst.

Suddenly, two men came up to accost her; one in front and one behind. She looked up to the sky and asked, "How about these guys?"

"Are you talking to us, beautiful one?" Asked one of the men.

She continued; "send me a sign..." Her eyes implored for a response which never came. She headed for a dark alleyway, the men followed her without fear, but above all without knowing what was at stake; she smirked. Her instincts took over, she wouldn't be able to stand up to them, not on her own.

When she'd found a place sufficiently far down the alley, she turned around. This surprised them.

"What are you doing, taking a walk here alone at night... you know it's not safe," said one of the men.

She looked up at him, her eyes had become as black as hell. She tilted her head to the right, taking a quick look at his neck. Then she looked straight at him, mouth slightly open. The face of the man turned to white. He could no longer speak, he could no longer yell out. The other man looked at this scene before making a run for it. Amused, she watched him flee, then paid her attention to the man remaining. He was terrified and he had good reason to be. She had nothing human left, except for that beauty, strange and dangerous...

"I'm going to liberate you from your fears, never more you will make others suffer," she said calmly, a touch of madness in her voice.

Faster than lightning, she threw herself on him, quenching her thirst all the while that the life was slipping away from the man's body. Then she abandoned the body behind a rubbish bin and went back.

Adrian let go of my hand, we were once again back here in this austere room. But what was she doing? Being lonely, she was acting like a young vampire, and that's what she thought she was: alone! She was still attached to her old life of a recluse in the convent, but she now had the feeling of having received a message from God; a mission. We had to save her and bring her back among us.

I started to read again, while Adrian was catching his breath a bit. I didn't want to lose any precious seconds on our case.

Wednesday
I'm not perfect and I don't recognise myself. I'm cleansing this world of impure souls and God knows they're here. The city is crawling with vermin, it's so easy to kill them. They are so naive, so nasty and so perverse. Human degradation in all its glory. I'm going to rest, and tomorrow I'll be back here again. Not to harm the nice people, but to purify the world of the bad ones.

I raised my eyes again towards Adrian. There was nothing written on the notebook.

"Tomorrow is now today, she's in town. We have to go there," I said, getting up.

"And where are you going to go? We don't know where she is, Lilly. Sit down please."

"You told me you have the power to sense us. Can't you find her then? Sensing like you did for me?"

"It's still too soon, she's a vampire like any other. It's like finding a needle in a haystack. We're going to try a viewing and find her that way."

"Okay."

No sooner had I finished my words than my hands were already positioned for another viewing, but this time in the present.

Adrian came to join me. He looked exhausted.

"Do you feel well?"

"Yes, I'm well, please don't worry."

"Alright, but I still worry even so! What's the matter?"

"After several teleportations in the same day, it tires you out, believe me."

"Do you want to feed yourself on me?" I asked, as if it were the most natural thing in the world, holding out my wrist to him.

He gave me a funny look of mingled surprise and craving.

"Go ahead," I insisted.

"Very well," he said, simply, delicately planting his fangs in my wrist.

I felt just a little sting, this was the first time during my Recouvrance that I'd offered my blood spontaneously. I knew it would help us to carry out our task more quickly.

After a few minutes, he stopped and stroked my wrist, thanking me.

"We can start again now," he told me.

Then we resumed our communion to try to find Laura.

We found ourselves this time by a railway line, judging by the regular train noise, like something musical reaching our ears. Laura was walking along the tracks, we were following her; if only she could sense us...

In the end, she found herself in a town which was unknown to me. It was full of people, a multitude of sounds were coming from all around; for the moment she was still peaceful. She didn't seem tired from the walk.

Logically, we arrived at a station. She looked all around and started to become agitated; the day was done. A man bumped into her in the bustle of the station, she now seemed lost.

She began running to escape the crowd, and left the station. The rain had made its appearance too. She took the first left turn, apparently to the red light district. For her, this was the ideal place for her mission! The hunt could now begin, she was spoilt for choice.

She paced the streets, walking in her slow, nonchalant manner. Looking all around her, entering into people's minds to find out who deserved to die that night. Tempted by several women begging for a merciful release, Laura resigned herself not to take herself for God. It was not her job to save others and feeling pity would change nothing here. Speeding up her pace, she continued on her way.

She walked into a bar which had a dark red frontage; black curtains were concealing the interior. A man on the way in, acting as doorman, stepped aside to let her pass. She gave a slight smile by way of thanks, but didn't open her mouth. Her body had begun its metamorphosis.

Inside, the electric atmosphere could be intensely felt, reflecting the perversity of the men who came here to satisfy their bestial need for everything which they either didn't, or did no longer, dare to ask from their wives. There were also those for whom life had only brought solitude. She didn't linger on the latter.

At the end of the room where many humans were drinking, smoking and laughing, Laura spotted a staircase. No one paid any attention to her presence there. She went up the stairs, this was the floor which would be the theatre for her play.

Slowly, she walked past the bedroom doors, allowing her hand to trail along the red flock-covered walls. Lots of groaning, simulated or not, was issuing from the rooms. These pleasures didn't in the least bit interest Laura, who wasn't here for that.

Some sounds which were different from the rest, were emanating from one of the rooms some distance away. She could sense pain. A recent suffering. A victim too young to be here. Laura felt a much more intense anger taking over within her. She put her ear to the wall, because she had to be sure. She couldn't permit any mistake in her task. Closing her eyes, her hands both placed on either side of the door posts, she relaxed her neck; she had reached her destination. The screams from inside were being muffled. This must stop.

She slowly opened the door, darkness reigned in the room; candles here and there struck an unreal and jarring note to what she was hearing. What a masquerade, she thought! On the bed was lying a young, much too young, girl being crushed by the body of a hideous man, panting and taking an unrequited and stolen pleasure. The young girl was crying. With each sob, he struck her a staggering blow in the pelvis.

Laura approached the bed. The young girl saw her. She sensed coming from her, a mixture of shame, guilt and terror; she motioned to her to be quiet, by putting her finger to her lips and letting out a discreet *"shhh"*. Too busy with his dirty work, the man didn't notice. In one swift motion, too fast to be detected, Laura threw him across to the other side of the room. Then she stood in front of him, legs apart, as if to show him her dominance.

She said to the girl, without turning around:

"Get yourself dressed, flee and never come back here."

Terrified, the girl didn't budge.

"Right now!" she shouted.

She heard her get up with difficulty, gather her clothes and sneak out through the window. The sound of the fire-escape ladder let her understand that she could finally deal with the man. This night, she will have saved two souls. She thought to herself; from way up there, will he be proud of me? She crouched down in front of the man, staring hard at him. He was now pale.

"You're less cocky now, huh?" She said.

The man wasn't able to answer. She saw him look at the door.

"Don't even think about it," she said, smiling.

She intentionally left a silent pause to accentuate his fear and then carried on:

"Your hour has come."

The man tensed up, and leaned against the wall, realising that his life truly was at stake. He managed to open his mouth to let out a "Mercy!" He lowered his gaze. She grabbed his head by the hair and brought herself up close to his face.

"Don't worry so much, it will be very quick, since, as you see, I'm very thirsty."

Tears streamed down the man's face, but it would take more than that for Laura to take into account this insignificant and worthless detail. The girl's tears had led her to him. Those of the torturer don't attract any mercy. She tilted her head to the side, his jugular was bulging; she could see there the beating of his heart. She ran her tongue over her teeth as if to assure herself that all of this was real. Then she sank her fangs with all her might into the man's flesh, who let out a yell for a fraction of a second.

With each intake of blood, she felt the warmth permeate her body, the man becoming no more than a puppet in her hands. She bit him again with even more ferocity, emptying him of the little vital essence he had left. Then she let him go, he collapsed on the floor. She stood back up; strangely, she didn't seem to feel full. She headed over to the window and sat on the sill, looking down. Who knows, could she send another gift to heaven? She didn't have to wait long, someone spoke to her:

"What are you doing perched up there?"

She turned her head towards the voice and let herself delicately drop, to land on the ground in front of the man who had forced his destiny by speaking to her. He made a move of recoil, surprised at a fall of two floors having posed no difficulty for this girl. He wanted to flee, but this was to be otherwise.

"I was waiting for you," she replied, in a charming voice.

The man gave her a funny grin. She was now walking gently around him, putting him ill-at-ease. She could detect fear in him, but also a strong maliciousness. She put her hand on his shoulder, which startled him.

"Don't touch me," he said.

"Haven't you come here for that?" She whispered in his ear.

The man frowned.

"You're scary, but you intrigue me."

He began to gain in confidence. Leaning back against the wall, she was happy to let him come over to her, wanting perhaps to play with him a little before killing him. Laura's smile had the effect of giving additional reassurance to the man, who came towards her and placed himself within inches of her body. She immediately felt a repulsion. With one swift movement, she reversed the roles by pinning him up against the wall, his smile being instantly wiped from his face. She pressed herself up to him, looking him up and down, making him feel very uncomfortable. He tried to get out of her grip, but she held him there still.

"Are you afraid of one weak woman?"

Then she was taken with laughter, annoying the man, who had been challenged in his manhood. With one hand, she lifted him a few inches off the ground. The man struggled as much as he could, trying to give her a few kicks.

"Is that it, can't you do better than that? In this case, I'll cut short your terror; goodbye friend!" She exclaimed.

She put him down and threw herself on him savagely, emptying him so quickly of his blood that she was surprised herself. She let go of the body and watched it slide onto the ground, she didn't even take the trouble to hide it.

This was so dangerous and irresponsible!

Laura finally made her way back. Straight in front of her, she didn't want to stop any more now, she just wanted to be back home. Speeding up her footsteps to reach the station, she took the last train leaving for her village. She sat down and watched outside, the train was going along quickly. The man facing her was staring at her oddly. She stared hard at him.

"Go and sit somewhere else, for your own good!" She virtually begged him.

Then she turned her attention to the scenery; meanwhile he had listened to her and gone to sit on another seat.

Adrian cut the link, she was coming back now.

"She killed the second man for pleasure, she wasn't obliged to. She's lost. We must intervene."

"That's what we're here for, Lilly. Before it's too late..."

He paused awhile.

"Before she makes things any worse for herself too, because then it will be more difficult to wake her up."

"How can one lose their humanity in such a short time? I do not understand this violence."

"For her it's a mission; on one side there is God and on the other, the humans. She's between two worlds; that of the humans and the early stages of her Recouvrance. Her state of being a vampire, which she doesn't perhaps understand very well even if she does however seem to accept it, and her hunger to satisfy it. Nobody is there to help her, so she falls back on her last human convictions. She excuses herself, so to speak, by saying that God led her down this path for a good reason.

"Yes, but that violence in her eyes, in her approach to the humans. Does God really tolerate such acts?"

"She uses the powers which were given to her, charm and temptation, to achieve her ends. As to whether God condones it or not, it doesn't matter, knowing whether she will be able to bear her actions; that's another story."

"Her aim is only death," I said, sadly.

"No, her aim, her mission as she believes it, is the purification of the impure. For her, these actions are justified."

"What will happen now?" I asked.

I was still shocked by what we had just directly experienced.

"We'll bring her back on the right path. We're going to re-awaken her conscience and continue her Recouvrance, that way she'll regain her proper place. Just like you're in the process of doing this yourself."

"Yes, I sincerely hope so."

"You know, Lilly, each of your Recouvrance are different, and you don't all get the chance to meet someone like Darren."

I set myself thinking about him. What would have happened if I'd met another vampire; less straight, more wild? I didn't dare imagine such a scenario, not after what I'd just seen!

"Do you think we'll find Lusiana?" I asked.

"Lou and Agor are working on that."

"I hope she's alright."

"Me too."

Adrian put his hand on my arm.

"Here she is, be quiet."

Then, he got up and positioned himself behind the door. I would be the first thing that Laura would see on entering the room. How would she react?

She opened the door warily, she must have sensed us, just like we ourselves had done her. In a split second she was there, pinning me against the wall. I'd barely had time to react and stand up. With a sharp kick, Adrian closed the door with his foot.

She stared hard at me with that same crazed look.

"What are you doing in my home?" She shouted.

"We've come looking for you Laura," I replied, as calmly as possible.

Adrian made a gesture, I motioned for him not to move.

"I don't know you!"

She ended her sentence by planting her fangs into my shoulder. She'd done exactly what I'd hoped she would do. The magic worked immediately. The images arrived at a hundred miles an hour into my head.

The fusion was working, I was getting my sister back, more and more as the images filed past. I felt a disarray overwhelming her, in the face of her actions, whilst seeing once again these moments that we'd shared, but I felt also a great joy and an immense relief coming from her, relief at not being the monster she thought she was.

Her fangs still planted there, she wasn't now sucking my blood; only this contact remained. She wanted to know more, not to cut off the sharing. Right now, she was hungry for knowledge. Her Recouvrance could at last actually begin, we were nourishing ourselves on our memories, in conjunction with each other. She was suspended from my neck, and I didn't budge until the moment when she finished by placing her head on my shoulder. Slowly, as if for a child, I wrapped my arms around her and placed my hand on her hair. Everything was happening very quickly, much quicker than with Lou or Agor during the council. They probably know how to manage the flow, they know how to measure out their gifts, which wasn't the case for Laura and myself. I was feeding my memory with what she offered wholesale, and letting her take from it what she wanted.

It was intoxicating.

Laura was my younger sister. The youngest, the one who must be protected, because psychologically she was much weaker, but with the same physical strength which we all possessed. And we had to have strength to live how we live, and this has been so through the centuries.

We were very much linked, but I'd felt that for a long time already. This fusion would just bring me back the memories of our past, but even without this sharing I knew I loved her more than the others. We were alike, my mother had seen it clearly when she asked me to take care of Laura, at the moment when she was falling into her sleep. Lou hadn't sent me here for nothing, I was the best placed to help my sister.

She let go her grip.

"Lilly, have you come to my rescue?" She whispered.

"We've come here for you, yes" I replied

She turned around and saw Adrian, who had observed the whole scene in silence, respectful of this unique moment. She walked over to him.

"Hello Adrian, sorry for that dramatic entrance."

"Hello Laura, it's been a long time since I've seen you. It's pleasing to see that you still have all your strength," he said, to lighten the mood.

"Always so funny, the Orkani," she replied, taking him in her arms.

They already knew each other well, it would seem.

"I think it's time to go home," she announced, looking at the room.

She put her few belongings into a bag, and began frantically rummaging all around.

"Is this what you're looking for?" Adrian asked, handing her ring to her.

She almost snatched it from his hands.

"Yes! Thanks." she said, slipping away it carefully.

She seemed a little embarrassed by her outburst; this ring had some importance for her. So why then had she removed it?

"I have to say goodbye to the priest."

"Yes, we'll be waiting outside for you," I said.

"Okay, don't leave without me, hey! She insisted, jokingly.

"Certainly not," quipped Adrian.

Laura was watching me with tenderness, as we left the enclosure through the gardens, and as she headed over to the rectory. Several long minutes later, she joined us again. We could now return, against all expectations; things had happened quite quickly in the end.

Adrian teleported us one by one; firstly Laura, who had no need at all to find herself alone again, even for a few seconds; and lastly me. During the moments of our dematerialization journey, I was imagining coming back home and seeing Darren, but that wasn't the case. We found ourselves in Brussels at Lou's place.

This time, the first thing I did was to be sick. This second trip had shaken me up; or has it been all those events? It mattered little; the result was here. It made Adrian burst out laughing; less so Lou, seeing the state of her rug. I apologized quickly for it. But it was only a little blood.

"I thought I'd be coming back to my place," I said, sadly.

"Soon, Lilly, I'd like us all to take stock of the situation," said Lou.

"Okay."

"Let's go to the council room, the conference system is better there," she announced, heading towards the basement of the building.

We followed her without saying a word.

13. Progress

The room seemed completely empty with just the four of us there. The others were participating from their places of residence. I heard the greetings of each one; the one from Darren came right into my heart, I missed him terribly.

"Hello!" Began Lou, "first of all, I'd like to thank you all for being able to join us. That said, let's get to the point: some news is happy, some rather disturbing. The first good news is Laura's return; Lilly and Adrian's mission was a real success," she said, smiling at us.

"Thanks to you both," Laura intervened.

She was radiant, but would she manage to forget what she'd gone through in Madrid? I'd only been a spectator and it had been hard for me. So what about for her?

"Lizzy, how have things been going with you? Did you find Polvus? Could you talk to him?" Lou continued.

"Hello everyone, yes I've seen him. He granted me an audience, but this wasn't easy. These wizards are really strange. In brief, I know why Albert died, and I fear that this was entirely his fault unfortunately."

"Explain yourself, Lizzy."

"Before his Recouvrance, Albert was with the Wizards. He was responsible for many tasks, one of which was to watch over an object, a kind of sacred stone in their eyes. Albert had accomplished this task with gusto, but he was overzealous! Firstly, he hadn't wanted to return this stone, which was the reason the wizards' first attack against him came, the time that Lilly and Darren went to save him in Scotland, a few months ago. Alas, his stupidity didn't stop there," she sighed. "He had cast a spell on the stone and none of the wizards had managed to remove the enchantment. And as you might have expected, in order to remove the enchantment, death was their only recourse."

"Why not ask Albert to remove the enchantment?" I asked.

"Because he lost all his powers of sorcery at the moment of his Recouvrance. A vampire can't be a wizard and vice versa," she clarified.

I looked at Adrian, who in my opinion was a bit of a wizard. Anyway, there was magic in him, certainly different, but nevertheless present.

"Only his death could liberate the object," reiterated Lizzy.

A heavy silence reigned in the room and no further sound came from the speakers. Albert had sealed his fate himself, the day of his Recouvrance.

How could he have imagined that the wizards would abandon it?

Now that we know the reasons for the death of Albert, we could concentrate ourselves on Moonroe and his clique.

But Lou had indicated to us that the wizards owed us one life - a life for a life – this fact couldn't be forgotten.

The wizards hadn't acted with fair play towards us, the vampires! They had killed one of our own, an Imhumvamp and furthermore, on the other hand they had divulged vital information about us to a human, thus putting us in danger. This could not go unpunished.

For now, Moonroe remained our priority. With that, Lou continued by questioning Agor.

"Agor has news concerning Lusiana, so I'll leave it to him to tell you about it himself."

"Do you remember what Alexandre had announced to us? Moonroe had four names," he began.

"Yes, but not that of Lusiana," Alexandre intervened.

"No, that's correct, but that of Laura and her place of residence, yes. We can thus assume that he tracked Laura down, and that it was Lusiana who he seized, perhaps believing she was Laura."

"Knowing my sister, I would go more for the following version: in order to save Laura, Lusiana let herself get caught. It all depends on the number of attackers there were facing her," said Armon.

"You're absolutely right Armon. I know barely any human capable of mastering our sister. She'd have to have done it to protect Laura," nodded Agor. "Still, it's him who's holding her, and so we must act. Whereabouts are you in France with Moonroe?" He asked.

A click could be heard on the line; Darren spoke.

"The conference takes place tomorrow evening in Boulogne at the HQ of Immortalis Sangus. I managed to get an appointment with him at four o'clock," he said.

"Had that been easy?" I asked.

"Yes, he remembered me perfectly well," he replied.

"Is he still as crazy in his intentions?"

"He was calm on the phone, but cheerful at the idea of meeting me again."

"You'd made a good impression on him the first time," I added, smiling.

A smile which he could only guess at.

"Yes, but he's still seeking glory. We'll see what he's inclined to reveal to me."

"How do you plan to go about imposing Philip into his team, Darren?" asked Lou.

"I've prepared a series of questions which will completely naturally lead me to introduce Philip as a "Chemist", but the idea will have to seem to come from himself if we want this to work," he added.

"Okay," Lou concludes. "So to summarise; everything's happening around Moonroe now, because it all comes back down to this one man. However, I ask you to act with the utmost caution, because even if Lusiana let herself be taken, she is nevertheless still captive. And we don't know under what conditions!"

"What are we going to do to release her?" Laura asked.

"For the moment nothing, we must await the interview. When you're in the vicinity, you'll be able to feel Lusiana and we'll therefore know more about her condition. Darren, I suggest you find yourself someone to be the soundman or cameraman. The two of you, you'll be stronger and above all, also safer. We must be cautious."

"Yes, you're right, it's a good idea. I'll ask Vic to join me," he said.

"Who is Vic?" She asked.

"A friend of mine, a member of my group. I can vouch for him like my brother," he added proudly.

"Don't you miss the music, Darren?" Lou questioned.

"Yes! Because it helps me in many ways. Besides, this evening it's concert time at the club. If you could let me have my Lilly back, it would do her a lot of good as well."

"Of course Darren. I'll keep Laura with us instead. She needs peace for her Recouvrance, as well as Adrian," she said.

She turned to the latter.

"Return Lilly to her home please, Adrian."

"Of course," he said, getting up.

He headed over to me.

"If you want to say goodbye, now's the time."

I nodded and went to kiss Laura and Lou.

"See you soon everyone," I added, for the rest of the group.

Adrian took my hand to teleport me to the chateau. I was finally going to see Darren again. The point of arrival was the same as the one used a few days earlier for departing. Darren was there. I held Adrian in my arms, whispering:

"Thanks for everything, take care of my sisters, will you?"

His gaze brought me the answer, then he disappeared in a cloud of smoke. I threw myself into the arms of Darren. No feeling sick nor any nausea whatsoever, I felt too good for that. We stayed entwined for several minutes, filling our bodies with the heat of one another, with that serenity which being loved can bring.

"If you like, we can stay here this evening, Lilly," Darren whispered.

"No, I need to unwind, to spend a normal evening with you and my friends."

"As you wish, in this case without wanting to press you, we have to get ourselves ready, because it's already late," he finished by saying, smiling.

I acquiesced, placing a kiss on his mouth, and ran to have a shower. I put on some jeans and a pullover, the same clothes as one of the first times I was brought to the *Blood Blues Jazz Club*, his jazz club.

Fifteen minutes later, I found myself back downstairs waiting.

"You did that quickly," he said, taking his jacket.

"Yes, I know how to do that too," I replied, laughing.

We left the chateau, holding each other's hands.

14. An Evening like any Other

The journey to the club seemed quick to me, I was so happy with this evening. Darren and I were going out like before, like when he'd transformed me. That time seemed so distant now, and yet only a few months had passed, as though it was yesterday.

Barely had the car been parked, when I got out. Darren was staring at me from the other side.

"You seem so happy, Lilly."

"If you knew how much this event is timely," I confessed, "I need it, need to find myself here, to listen to you, to drink a beer and to think about nothing, other than to wonder what the next song will be."

"Spain; was it so tough?" He asked, as he skirted around the car to join me on the pavement.

I buried my gaze into his.

"Dreadfully, yes. I learned a lot, but I also saw what we were able to do in our worst moments."

"I'm here," he said tenderly, taking me in his arms.

"Yes, I know and I'm so glad to have you. No matter what; the vampire, whether young or in the course of Recouvrance, needs a good progenitor. This, which you told me once, makes complete sense now. If a '*bad*' vampire had transformed me, things would be different. Although in the end, I would have perhaps found out about everything, since after all, I'm still what I am. The road would just be longer and more painful."

I again placed a kiss on his lips, which he'd half-opened. Overwhelmed by our icy heat, I was losing myself, when...

"Hey! The two lovebirds," shouted Vic.

One last tender look to Darren and I ran over to Vic.

"My friend, I've missed you," I told him, hugging him warmly.

Arm in arm, we were returning to the club. There were barely ten minutes before the start of the concert. The club was full, it was a long time since they'd played, and the announcement about the resumption of their concerts had had its effect. Luckily my place at the bar was free.

While Darren headed to the stage and with Vic behind the counter, I was sitting on the same bar stool as on the first day. Except that things had changed, Marie wouldn't come tonight to interrupt the concert; this idea saddened me, but that's how it was. We couldn't change anything. I still felt soothed by being there. Now, I had memories here, and that's what enabled people to survive in death, our memories.

Vic placed a Corona in front of me without my having to order it. With a smile, I thanked him and let my eyes scan around the room.

At that moment, I noticed Philip by a table, a tray in hand. He was working here now, Vic certainly had his head screwed on. I knew I'd made the right choice in saving this rather curious man. I gave him a wave by way of a greeting, to which he responded deftly with one hand, holding the tray of glasses with the other.

All the tables were occupied, the bar was doing well with or without the concert. This place was a pleasant one.

As usual, Darren took his place on the left of the stage. The concert could begin. With the lights dimmed, the room had the most intimate air, we were in an atmosphere conducive to Jazz.

The sound of the saxophone filled my head, I was appreciating more and more this kind of music, so different from what I usually listen to. I let myself be carried away by the melody, thinking of nothing.

Vic brought me out of my reverie by changing over my glass, which I had emptied without even realising it, I smiled at him.

"How are you?" I asked.

"I'm fine. We returned yesterday from Ireland."

"Where did you put all their belongings?"

It had taken some time to sort everything out and pack it away. To many, they would have needed a good fortnight.

"In the basement of the castle. At an opportune moment, Darren can sort it through."

"And the house?"

"All closed up. He hasn't taken any decision on a possible sale."

"It's still too early, too fresh as well," I added, taking a sip of beer.

Someone at the bar called to Vic, he apologised to me and went to serve the customer. One question kept running through my head; I turned towards Darren.

"Darren, excuse me, but..." I began.

"Yes?"

"Does Vic know who I am?"

"*Yes, Martin informed him when he returned to Ireland to see Albert's remains. Why?*"

"*The question was nagging at my mind, I wanted to make sure, because I'm aware that we need to remain discreet, we Imhumvamps. I'm glad he's aware.*"

It always surprised me that Darren could chat with me and still stay focused on the music.

"*I understand, I know you're close. If Martin hadn't done it, I would have asked him to.*"

"*Thanks Darren. Oh! Another thing.*"

"*Yes, I'm listening.*"

"*I'm not bothering you?*"

"*No, you never bother me, whatever thing I'm doing, you're my priority...*"

"*How I love you!*"

"*Were you worrying about that?*"

"*No, no.*"

He could see me smile from where he was.

"*Is Vic okay to accompany you to see Moonroe tomorrow?*"

"*Yes he's going to accompany me, I'll make him aware of everything. So you can discuss the matter with him. You know, Vic's my blood brother and we've been friends for a few years now. He's much more to me than my right arm, you understand? So he knows everything.*"

"*Yes I know, thank you.*"

I saw him put his saxophone down, this was the break.

He joined me back at the bar, while the rest of the group as usual were using this little down-time to quench their thirst or smoke a cigarette.

"If I'd known you were about to be stopping, I wouldn't have bothered you," I said, welcoming him close to me.

"No, it was fine. I like to do several things at once, you know that," he replied, cheerfully.

I looked at him. We were here like normal people passing a nice quiet evening. An evening like any other, in short.

The time passed very quickly.

They played some jazz classics for another hour and, to finish, a few blues tunes. For the last few, Darren took over from the regular pianist, who took the microphone. I like Darren to sing. He does do it so well. It was good that he was diversifying though, and the audience too seemed to see it from my point of view.

As for me, I had discussed with Vic about what was going to happen the next day. The interview with Moonroe, the search for Lusiana, all these things where I couldn't take part because Moonroe knew my face.

I didn't divulge to him any of my own plans, he would be rather busy with his own things.

We parted in good spirits. We'd be seeing each other again in a few hours anyway.

I spent the night huddled against Darren, we had to be in good form tomorrow; a long day was awaiting us.

15. Immortalis Sangus

Everyone was busy, except for me. I had no role in the scenario which was going to play out in two hours' time. Darren and Vic made a perfect team, and Hector was going to be their driver.

Darren had categorically refused any help from me, even during the preparations. Powerless, I was only there to watch what they were doing. What only served to amplify my anger yesterday, was when he announced my eviction from the project. According to them, I was someone else to be concerned with, and they already had enough to think about without me. No slackening would be permitted for them. At least that's how I'd interpreted this bad news.

"Everything okay, Lilly?" Darren asked me.

"Yes everything's fine thanks," I replied with an air of contrariness; as if I was okay!

He looked hard at me.

"Don't ask me to pretend. I'm here to observe you. You will go, and me; I will stay here, worrying and knowing nothing. And you want me to be alright!"

"He knows you! Be reasonable, for God's sake!"

"I would still have been able to help you here. I don't know, there's always something to do. Couldn't I just load the van? I'm not impotent, you know!"

He came over to me with an air of sorrow.

"I know that. Forgive me," he said, lifting up my head.

Tears welled up in my eyes and he could see it very clearly. My anger became sadness. He pulled me to him and hugged me.

"I promise you will be aware of everything at each stage of our mission. I promise you," he finished by saying, placing a kiss upon my lips.

I kissed him back, drowning in tears.

"I know. Forgive me. This is our first real dispute, I think," I added.

"Yes you're right. But it's justified, trust me."

"'I'm going up to the bedroom for a bit, to calm down, if you don't mind?"

"Yes, I'll call you when we're ready to go."

"Okay, thanks."

With those words, I left for our bedroom. I closed the door behind me and took a few breaths, I didn't like disputes even when they were feigned.

"You were perfect, Lilly."

"No, I don't like lying to him," I said, as I turned to my sister Lou.

"I know that very well, don't worry, he'll understand. In the worst case, I will make him understand. Have you clearly understood all that you must do?" She asked.

"Yes of course. While they're doing their interview; me, I'll go and look for Lusiana, release her, and bring her back here."

"You know why you, alone, can do this, don't you?"

"Yes, I now know this. We're twins and our bond is so strong that even if she's unconscious, I'll be able to sense her. I saw her in Laura's memories in Madrid."

"Do you feel you're able to do it?" Lou asked.

"Absolutely, I prefer this, than to stay here to mope. It's time for me to retake my place."

She handed me a bag.

I opened it to discover a blonde wig and some clothes. My outfit was elegant and above all functional. I was going have to use my charms and my strength to succeed in my plan.

It was going to be necessary to enter the place without arousing suspicion, and to be able to move around inside as discreetly as possible, without being let down by my outfit. Along with Darren, I'd looked at the plans for the building. Lusiana could be anywhere, if they were keeping her there. The only places that I would have to avoid were Moonroe's office and the conference room; the only two rooms that could logically host the interview.

I heard Darren calling me; it was time. I turned to Lou to say goodbye, but she had gone.

Within a few seconds, I found myself on the front steps of the castle. Vic and Hector were waiting in the van. I gave them a wave, to which they responded with a smile, before I turned towards Darren.

"Be careful please. You know about Moonroe, and more, so now over time he's maybe stronger and more organised. Of this organisation, we don't know very much; we know nothing in fact," I said, snuggling myself up against him.

I wanted to tell him Lou's plan, but I couldn't take the risk of it all going kaput. If he knew, Darren would be capable of cancelling the mission to protect me, and of that there was no question. My sister needed me and we needed the information they would be gleaning from Moonroe.

"I'll be careful, we'll all be. We'll be back here in a few hours."

"Okay, have a good journey."

I grabbed him by the arm as he started to go down the steps.

"I love you, don't forget this," I added.

"I love you too," He said, with an odd look.

It was time to let him go before he could read my mind and discover my intentions.

I watched them go away and out through the gate. It was three o'clock in the afternoon. Plenty of time for me to prepare myself, which I did in record time. I was unrecognisable! I don't even know if Darren could recognise me if I accidentally bumped into him down a corridor.

It took me an hour and a quarter to get to the building of the "*Immortalis Sangus*" association. I noticed the van alongside the building, Hector was at the wheel. I looked up towards the sky, the tower seemed endless. The interview had been underway for thirty minutes now.

I stared at the front door and with a sure step, decided to make my way inside. I would have to be cautious and alert, yet smiling all the while.

The hall was gigantic, white and very bright. It had artificial light, with a conditioned and sanitised air like in a laboratory, a colossal laboratory in plain sight of everyone.

People were walking in all directions.

The reception desk was located in front of me, a young woman was waiting. She started to smile as I approached.

"Hello Miss, welcome to "*Immortalis Sangus.*" What may I do to help you?"

Her speech was well rehearsed. How many times a day did she repeat that phrase?

"Hello, I phoned this morning. I'm a biology student and I'd like to have access to your library to finalise my thesis, please."

"Of course, what's your name, please?"

"Anaïs Mansard," I said, quite naturally.

"Oh yes, you're on my list, welcome Miss Mansard. Here's your badge to get around," she said, offering me the precious pass.

I clipped it onto my jacket prominently.

"The library is located on the ninth floor, the elevators are on your left in that small corridor. I hope you find what you need."

"Yes, thanks," I added, heading off down to the corridor she'd told me about.

I pressed the call button for the elevators, there were four of them. For the time being, if my sister was here, I couldn't sense her. I entered the first one which arrived, its twelve buttons all were numbered apart from the last, where it was assigned as "*private.*" I strongly doubted that my sister was there. I pressed the number nine. The elevator stopped on the fifth floor and let a man in, a man who I recognised immediately; I'd seen him in one of my visions with Darren. The one in the cave!

Most fortunately, he couldn't recognise me. I'd not payed attention to the faces of the men that Darren had killed in the barn. If that had been the case, I would have known then that one of them hadn't taken part in Albert's death; he'd been replaced.

He pressed button ten, one floor above the library. This might be a good clue to locate Lusiana.

I walked out of the elevator, bowing politely, he didn't look very friendly. I found myself directly in the library; to my right a small office with a guard, who asked me to sign the visitors' register.

I began to walk around the aisles of books, pretending to be interested. Some other people were there, either sitting or looking for a book like I was doing! The room was very quiet. The only sounds that could be heard were those of pages being turned, pens scribbling, and that of a few footsteps.

I took a book from the "*human biology*" shelf and sat at a nearby table. Now, I needed to concentrate on my sister.

My first connection wasn't one which I wanted; it was into Darren's head that I'd introduced myself. I was very surprised, I had no choice but to talk to him. This kind of intrusion was palpable, especially for him.

"*How are things going, Darren?*" I asked, innocently.

"*Lilly? Where are you?*"

"*At the chateau, where would you like me to be?*"

"*We can't communicate from so far away, Lilly! Where are you?*"

"*Well here's the evidence we can do, Darren. So how's it going?*"

"*He's interested in meeting Philip.*"

"*Good, very good. Is that all?*"

Next, there followed a silence; I imagined he was attentive to Moonroe's responses. I didn't insist, as this moment had been a close call, and so I tried to concentrate again on my sister.

A few seconds later, the connection with Lusiana was finally made! I could hear her thinking and I joined myself to her.

"Lusi, this is Lilly, answer me."

"Lilly?"

The sound was barely audible, I sensed she was weak.

"Tell me where you are so I can come and get you."

"No, it's too late."

This sentence made me angry, to the point of dropping the book I was supposed to be studying. The noise alerted the guard, who came over to me.

"Miss..."

He read the name on my pass.

"Mansard," he finished by saying, after a few seconds.

"Yes, I'm sorry to have dropped the book, sir," I said.

I needed to keep a low profile.

"Take care, please," he said, returning to his place.

A real prison this place, I thought.

"Lusi, it's not too late, I'm here."

"Don't take unnecessary risks," she said, painfully.

"On what level are they keeping you?"

"On the tenth floor, I can hear the sound of a boiler nearby."

"I'm coming! Hold on, I'm coming!" I pleaded.

"I'm going to try to," she eventually said, after a moment.

I stood up to put the book in its place. I pulled out my mobile; I'd had time to discreetly photograph the plans with Darren yesterday. I had to find another way than the elevator, to reach the floor above, and secretly so. Yes! There was an emergency exit, I just needed to successfully guide myself through the maze of aisles.

"You can't use a mobile phone here, it's prohibited. Please turn it off."

The voice of the guard behind me made me jump. I slowly turned to him, with an air of innocence.

"My mother is asking me where I am. Parents; you know what they're like," I said, with an air of boredom.

"Okay, but turn it off now, or I'll be obliged to confiscate it."

"There you are, that's done," I said, showing him that it was off.

"Good, I don't want to have to tell you again," he finally said, turning on his heel.

"Yes Sir," I muttered.

The emergency exit must be at the end of the room, near the windows. Softly, I approached it, I didn't want to get noticed now. It was to be found in the exact place I'd had the time to memorise. I opened it quietly; luckily there was no alarm, which was sometimes the case with this kind of door, such as in schools, for example. I gently closed it behind me.

I found myself on a concrete staircase, grey and sombre, with only the glow of the fire exit signs above the doors for illumination. A quick glance showed me that we could get back down to the ground floor by that route.

I took off my shoes in order to make less noise; the concrete was resonating a lot, and I had seen enough of that guard for today!

To reach the tenth floor was child's play. I was now right at the door. There was no sound behind it, except for that of the boiler as noted by Lusiana. I was close to my sister.

"Lilly... don't come in."

"I'm here, Lusi, a few yards away from you."

"No, it's too late for me, save yourself!"

"Out of the question. Save your strength for the escape."

I opened the door and put my head carefully through the opening to view the corridor; it was empty. There was no one there and no camera either. I left the door ajar, as it had no handle, a detail which I found strange for an emergency exit, but less strange if I were in a prison.

I was on my guard, I was tense. Listening out for the slightest noise, I walked cautiously toward the waves that my sister was giving off. I slipped along against the walls and finally arrived at a door behind which I could feel her presence.

Suddenly, a hand touched my shoulder, I turned around with a jump to face that cursed guard.

"What's your excuse this time, Miss Mansard? You're looking for the toilet perhaps?" He said, ironically.

It was too much this time, I stared right into his eyes. I gave him a little smile just as ironic as his last sentence, and then broke his neck in a split second. I deadened his fall as much as I could, when the radio made a noise.

"Rene, have you found the nosey one?"

I listened to the crackling of the radio. There would be hardly any time left before the other guards would arrive. I crushed the radio and threw it on the floor near the body.

"Lusi, protect yourself, I'm coming in now."

Silence filled my head. I kicked in the metal door, which gave way under my strength, amplified by my anxiety. Then I froze, petrified by what I saw.

Lusiana, my blood, my sister, was lying on a cold table identical to a post-mortem table. Several thin tubes were connected to her body. I couldn't even count them. What were they doing to her? Or rather what had they done to her? Nothing was emanating from her lifeless body.

I walked sadly over to her and began to remove the needles they had planted in her arms, her legs and her head. Her eyes were closed.

Tears streamed down my cheeks. I had arrived too late. I wasn't able to save her and she'd known I wouldn't have succeeded, she'd been conscious of it. I went over to her face and wanted to put a kiss on her forehead, but her skin burned me.

Looking around me, I grabbed a pair of gloves that had been placed on a tray of needles, and put them on. I leaned over her body, lifting her eyelids; a thin stream of silver flowed from her eyes.

They had emptied her of her blood, and then had poisoned her by filling her up again with silver. These people had known what they were doing.

Gradually, hatred replaced grief. I didn't have any remorse for the guard now. His death had been much less painful than my sister's, and much quicker too.

Quickly, I undid the bags of blood which were still suspended there, and put them into my bag. Some of it was missing; a woman's body contains about five litres of blood; these few bags didn't account for all of my sister's blood. Under no circumstances should they have this blood, under no circumstances should they be in possession of this enzyme, threatening our existence.

I didn't hear the alarm that was sounding throughout the building. I began to search the refrigerated cabinets in this room, and reclaim the missing bags. That done, I had to contact Darren.

"Darren, Lusiana is dead. They killed her."

"Where are you Lilly? This here, it's the signal for battle, I don't know what's going on, but…"

"I'm on the tenth floor," I interrupted him.

"How? We're coming!" He shouted, inside my head.

I looked at this cold room, deprived of windows, this torture chamber. Everything was so white, so clean, and yet my sister's body had been drained of blood. They hadn't lost a drop.

I heard footsteps fast approaching.

"Hello Lilly."

"Hello Doctor," I replied, turning to face him.

I took off my wig, it was making me hot, and anyway, it served no purpose now.

"You seem to be well," he said, as if nothing had happened.

"Much better than her, indeed," I replied, pointing the body of my sister.

"You see Lilly, some sacrifices are necessary," he began, as he approached the table where my sister's body lay.

I followed this man with my gaze: this man in whom I had put all my trust a few years earlier.

"And this one was inevitable," he said, stroking her face.

"Don't touch her," I cried, pushing him against the wall.

He smiled, without me knowing why. He should have been scared. He was mad, raving mad.

"Why keep it a secret for yourselves, this elixir which could save the human race?"

"Look around you, look at the things you do. Why should we give you what makes us who we are? Why should we give you this gift?"

With each question, I approached him a little more closely.

"You're not worth the trouble, Moonroe," I eventually said, a few inches from his face.

I feared nothing. He was alone and unarmed, and I was stronger than him.

"But Lilly, animals have always been part of medical experiments to improve our living conditions..."

"I'm not an animal, Moonroe!" I yelled, blocking him up against the wall now.

Undaunted, he continued his discourse, still on a condescending tone. He thought he was superior to us, and yet he wanted a part of us.

"So that we can live longer. Look at you! Some months ago you were just a rag, you could barely stand. You're not human! You're not so anymore! Look at you! Your eyes, your nails and your skin," he continued.

He paused for a moment, but I didn't let him go.

"You have the power of regeneration. You jump from one state to another with a click of your fingers. Nothing in nature can do that, apart from you Imhumvamps! You are extraordinary beings, Lilly."

"Then why are you striving to destroy us?"

"Because you're selfish. And I don't strive to destroy you, I just want this enzyme, but you're fighting against me. So I have no choice but to take what you forbid me to have."

His madness was far more advanced than we had feared.

"No! You take nothing except our lives. And this for the sole purpose of satisfying yourself, not the human race. You are mad, Moonroe, this hope of immortality has made you lose your mind!"

"What life, Lilly? You are dead!"

I stared at him, like I had never done before.

"I'll show you what animals are capable of doing."

With those words, I planted my fangs into his neck and drank of his madness like the animal he thought I was.

"So, Moonroe, how do you feel now that life is escaping your fragile human body?" I asked.

He opened his mouth but no sound came out. I saw the fear in his eyes now.

"And now; for her," I said, nodding towards my sister.

Again, my canines penetrated his skin, he began to lose control of his body, which was overcome by spasms.

"For Albert now; my brother who you killed for no reason," I cried.

For the third time, I fed on him. Soon he would be no more than an empty shell, but I wanted him to suffer one last time, so I stopped myself.

He was there at my mercy, like a puppet in my hands. He could barely keep his eyes open, but I wanted him to embrace death in full awareness. I took from my bag a packet of blood. I opened it and made him taste this enzyme that led to his death.

"That's what you want, so taste some!" I said, opening the bag and thrusting the tip into his mouth. The blood poured over him, he no longer had the energy to swallow.

Certainly it won't bring back his life, but it would give him back a little bit of breath to face his death. I smiled at him, taking his head in my hands.

"No, Lilly!"

I turned towards Darren at the moment when I felt Moonroe's head detach from his neck. The little blood which was left spurted out, and the rest of his body slumped onto the floor.

Albert, Lusiana and Marie had been avenged!

"I did what I had to do, Darren."

I saw Vic enter the room; his eyes went from Moonroe to Lusiana to me.

"Don't look at me like that, I'm not a monster!" I said.

Then my reflection appeared to me in the metal cabinet in front of me, I had blood everywhere. I approached it to see myself better. I turned towards them, letting go of Moonroe's head, which bounced and rolled across the floor near to his body.

"What have I done?"

Darren took me in his arms.

"You have eliminated an obstacle, Lilly, and avenged your family. There's nothing wrong with that."

"And Marie," I added.

"Yes Marie," he said, sadly.

All this was sad, all these unnecessary deaths. I regained the upper hand in seconds, this wasn't the time to feel sorry for our fate. We had to act before Moonroe's henchmen turned up and it all got worse. There had been enough victims for today.

Moving away from Darren, I spoke to them.

"We have to clean up and leave. I don't want to leave Lusiana here," I said, stroking her head with my gloved hand.

At that moment, Adrian landed in the room, followed by a man who I didn't know.

"Who are you?" I shouted.

Adrian positioned himself to face me.

"This is an Orkani, Lilly, Lusiana's one," he said, sadly. "I'd like to present Erik."

He prostrated himself before her. I went over to him, I placed my hand amicably on his shoulder.

"I'm sorry Erik, my condolences."

"Thank you, Lilly," he said, simply.

The instant afterwards, he disappeared in a cloud of smoke, carrying the body of my sister.

"How did you know we were here and in trouble, Adrian?" I asked.

"I asked Hector to contact him," said Darren.

"Ah! That's good. And now what shall we do with Moonroe's body?"

"I'll take care of that. I just have to find all the pieces. You didn't pull your punches!" Adrian announced.

He placed the head along with the open packet of blood into a bag. He asked me for the other packets and walked away, carrying Moonroe in his arms.

Some men were banging on the door, which Vic had blocked from the inside; there remained ahead for us shortly, a bloody confrontation.

"You must leave, Lilly, we'll deal with it," Darren commanded.

"But..."

"That's enough for you today, don't you think?" He said, pushing away the blood-matted hair from my face.

"Yes, you're right, but I can't just walk down the street like this."

"No, Adrian will come back here in a few seconds," he said.

Adrian arrived, took me in his arms without a word, and lifted me up. He put me down at the chateau where Amelie was waiting for me.

"Go back and get them, I know that it's exhausting for you, but please don't leave them there. Do it for me."

"Yes, Lilly, don't worry, that was the plan. I'm leaving you with Amelie; we'll soon all be back."

And he disappeared on those words.

I turned towards Amelie.

"Hello. We had a rough day."

"Yes, that's what I'm able to understand. How's Hector doing?" She asked.

I'd completely forgotten about Hector, but logically he would have been fine since he'd remained outside.

"He wasn't in the building with us, so I think he's doing well and will be on the way back. But driving takes a little longer. Doesn't he have a mobile phone?"

"No, he doesn't want one. It would be useful for a day such as this. In truth, at the chateau and the area around it, we communicate by thought," she added.

And it was correct that Hector never went out except on very rare occasions. I hoped he was well, with the utmost sincerely.

"I've prepared the bathroom for you, Lilly. I'll go and wait downstairs," she said, as she was leaving me.

"Thanks, Amelie".

The moment that I slid into the shower, I heard Adrian dropping Vic off in the kitchen. This made me smile, knowing that Vic was a little afraid of Amelie. I remained alert, awaiting the arrival of Darren. Which I didn't have to wait long for; I was relieved. The door to the bathroom opened slightly.

"Can I join you?"

"It's even rather recommended, if you don't want to trigger my anger."

"Oh! Hell no! I saw very well what you were capable of today," he added, snuggling against me.

"There's nothing funny about it, you know."

"I know, but apart from Lusiana, we are all well. You couldn't do anything more for her."

I didn't answer about Lusiana, because if the guard hadn't delayed me, maybe I could have saved her. But I knew in my heart that the only thing I could have done was to watch her die.

"Hector too?" I asked.

"Yes, he'll be here in an hour. When things got really aggravated, I asked him to leave."

Darren washed my hair gently, while we were talking. I enormously appreciated his tenderness at that moment.

"Thanks. Amelie was worried. You could offer Hector a mobile phone though!"

"But I already have done. It's still lying around in the kitchen, in its original packaging!"

"Ah!"

We stayed embracing for several minutes without saying anything, with only the sound of water breaking the silence, as it fell and washed away my conscience.

"Why is our life so hard, Darren?"

"For the most part because of the humans, I'm afraid."

"Why is theirs less so?"

"That isn't true. Their problems are different, that's all. The human is mortal, he falls ill. He risks his life at every moment; when he uses his car, lights a cigarette or even takes a swim. Fortunately, he doesn't really mind unless his life becomes a true nightmare."

"Yes, you're right. But why can't we manage to live with them?"

"If we could live in harmony with humans, then the world would be even better. It's a nice thought, Lilly, but there will always be a Moonroe somewhere that envies our immortality, our ability to move quickly and our strength. We can't trust them, not blindly anyway. But this harmony can also very well be broken by a vampire on a quest for blood. We're all meant to live, but not together, not yet. They're not ready and neither are we.

"Some are on both sides, I'm sure."

"A handful of individuals, little more."

He finished his sentence by kissing me. We heard Hector arrive, I sighed in relief.

Darren smiled at me now, handing me my robe.

"Come on, a good cup of coffee is needed."

"I'm coming... Darren?"

"Yes?" He said, turning around as he was about to open the door.

"Where is Alexandre?" I asked, putting on my clothes.

"At Lou's place with Martin."

"Why?"

"It was more prudent."

"Okay," I said, taking his hand.

As we arrived downstairs, our coffees were awaiting us, but this time they'd been prepared by Amelie, who was keeping Hector company in the kitchen. Darren headed straight for her.

"Hello Amelie, and thanks for looking after Lilly."

"It was nothing," she said, shyly.

For the first time, I could watch them talking. Hector held Amelie by her shoulder. It seemed to me that this made him equally happy. Darren tasted the coffee, all eyes were on him.

"You should make us coffee more often, Amélie; it's excellent, bravo!"

"I'll do it gladly."

Then she smiled at Hector.

Was she now reconciled with Darren?

Did the events of the day bring them closer?

Had they realised how precious life was and that a quarrel of several decades didn't signify very much?

I took my place with Darren, Vic joined us too, and for once allowed himself to be served.

16. The Key

The early summer hadn't been too hot and the flowers were spilling over into the aisles, much to the delight of Amelie.

No one had reproached me for killing Moonroe: even I'm not doing so any longer. He deserved what happened to him. The evening conference had been cancelled. Professor Moonroe had disappeared! The investigation was in progress, but certain rumours were saying that he had, this time, really lost his head.

Us, we knew very well that it was even truer than the humans could believe.

As agreed, all my belongings were repatriated to the chateau. The furniture had been donated to a charity, I had just kept the contents. This amounted to about thirty boxes full of books, DVDs and other diverse objects. The day before, I'd spent a lot of time putting everything in the places that Darren had arranged for me around the chateau.

He had even brought an identical desk to his, and put it in the library instead of the chair, where I'd sat one day, with the nagging questions. This room was now ours.

We were sitting now, him doing his accounts, me opening the last box that I still had left. This was the one where, when you move, they put all that's left over; in short, the most difficult one to sort out.

I made two piles on the floor: to my right, things that I would keep, and on my left those that were to be discarded. Every time I put a piece of paper or a little thing on the floor, Darren smiled.

Then I found a small box covered with brown leather and gently placed it on the desk. It intrigued me. It wasn't much larger than a shoebox. I ran my fingers over it, looking for a way to open it. After a few minutes, it started to annoy me; I rested against the back of my chair and sighed.

"Do you have a problem, Lilly?"

"I don't know how to open this thing," I replied, with a frown.

He got up to come over and examine my mystery box.

"Um, may I?" He asked, taking it in his hands.

"Of course, if you can open it, that suits me."

"Thanks, Lilly," he said, smiling.

He peered at it from every angle, turning it over and over. Then he smiled at me and I heard a little click.

"Over to you discover the content," he said, placing it in front of me.

"Oh, thanks. Stay close to me, please."

"As you wish, but I don't believe you risk anything, it's just a box," he added, chuckling.

"Don't make fun of me. I really thought that a spell was preventing me from opening it."

"Open it now, I'm curious to see what it contains!"

"Right, let's do it."

Much to my disappointment, the box was empty! At first glance anyway, because as I bent over, I noticed a piece of paper sticking out of the tiny right hand corner at the bottom, underneath the leather. Darren gave me a paper-knife, which he'd gone to get from his desk.

Carefully, I passed it beneath the leather and lifted up the false bottom. There was sitting there, a bank slip and a key. I took the key in my hand, it meant nothing to me. The bank was not my own, at least not that I could remember. I turned to Darren.

"What does this mean?"

"I don't know. I think we should go there for answers. This key is used to open a safe box."

"For me?"

"We will know there, on the spot."

I barely had time to get my bag, the key and the note before Darren was already dragging me into the car. He was even more curious than I was!

The bank was located in the first arrondissement of Paris, a small branch of the Agricultural Credit Bank. Funny name for a bank.

We parked on one of the reserved spaces for its customers. A security guard opened the door. We thanked him and headed towards the single counter.

I pulled the key out from my pocket and handed it to the young redhead who was sitting there, looking bored.

"Hello, I would like to access my safe box please."

"Hello, do you have any ID, please?"

"Of course," I replied, handing it to her.

She wrote my name on a register, smiled and stood up.

"Follow me, please."

We followed her down a cream marble corridor. We passed by several secure doors, to finally arrive in a room full of safe boxes. I didn't know which of these boxes was mine. Fortunately, she knew this.

She introduced her own key into the first lock and looked at me.

"Come on, you have to put your key into the lock and the safe box will open. I'll leave you to it. When you've finished up, please return my key. You have a table here. Take your time."

"Thank you, madam."

Then she disappeared. I positioned myself facing the lock and introduced my key, a clack was heard, and the door opened by itself.

"Here we go," I said to Darren, taking the drawer.

"Wait, I'll fetch it out."

"Thanks."

I had the strength to do it, but Darren was a gentleman. He put it on the table. I took a seat, he did likewise. We were facing a black box, which was longer than it was wide. What could it contain?

"Open it," he said, impatiently.

I looked at him.

"Darren, whatever we find in that box, promise me to..."

"Hush, Lilly, open it already."

"Okay."

I lifted the lid. I looked around inside it. It contained photos, letters and another pair of keys, which I picked up. The keys to a house without a doubt. Then I took hold of the picture, while looking at Darren.

"Do you know him?" I asked.

"Not at all. You seem intimate," he answered, simply.

The photo was of me, smiling at a man who was holding me in his arms; and yes we had been intimate, judging by our looks, Darren was right. I would have said that we loved each other. I turned the photo over, there was an inscription: Paris 1982.

"I don't remember him. I promise."

He put his hand over my mouth.

"I know that. Don't worry about it."

He took me in his arms and continued.

"Before me, you've had many lives, too. Now, at present, we are together. But we must not under any circumstances forget what made us who we are. That which made us stronger too. We lived, we loved. That's life."

"Yes, you're right," I said, stroking his cheek.

I looked at him lovingly. His words were sincere. He wasn't sad or jealous. He was just realistic.

"Still, I have no idea what happened in 1982."

"We'll find out, Lilly; you need to as well. I guess that if you kept these letters and pictures, it's because there must be a reason. And we'll discover it together, that reason; if you wish, of course."

"Yes, please, together we will find out."

I stayed contemplating all these things, when suddenly the words of Adrian came back to me.

"In Spain, Adrian told me something about Paris in 1982."

"How did you come to be talking about that period?" He asked.

"Because I told him I loved seeing mixed couples. It gave hope for humans and vampires living together without killing each other. The watchman there is married to a human," I replied, smiling.

"And what did he say about it?"

"That I would come back to my own point of view when I have finished my Recouvrance, and he mentioned that particular year."

I looked at the picture, which I still was holding.

"He's perhaps human?"

Darren could see that all this disturbed me. He picked up the keys and took the rest of the photos and letters and put them in my hand.

"Lilly; bring it all. We'll return to the chateau. We'll find the house which is opened by these keys. You're going to read the letters, and everything will come back to you."

"Okay."

I put everything in my bag. Darren put the drawer back in its place, then he locked it.

I gave the two keys to the young woman, because I had no more need of them, and we returned to the chateau.

I left a message for Adrian; I wanted to see him, to discover more about Paris in 1982, but for now, I didn't want to ruin my life or that of Darren, because of my past.

So I put everything into the brown leather box, which I left on my desk. If Darren wanted to read the letters, he could, I had no secrets from him. Then I took his hand and said:

"What would you say to a good film?"

"Very good idea, I'll let you choose, while I go and get some wood to make a small fire."

"Oh! Then a romantic evening deserves a romantic film."

"I fear the worst, suddenly."

"We will watch "*Pride and Prejudice.*" And you must keep your eyes open right until the end," I said, fixing him with my gaze.

He kissed me and went off to get some wood, while I set up a cozy corner in the living room.

17. Epilogue

I was walking peacefully in the grounds, my cats were following me everywhere. They had adopted the castle and its inhabitants. For the time being, they were sleeping at Amélie and Hector's place until the day that Darren would accept them being in with us, even after nightfall.

I heard the sound of a car which had stopped at the gate. The postman called to me.

"Hello, I have a registered package," he shouted from afar.

I went over to meet him, I could easily sign for Darren.

"Hello, who's this package addressed to?"

"Uh... Miss Mansard? Is that you?"

This detail shocked me. Who could be using this name to me?

Knowing that Moonroe was dead, it was rather strange to be sent a package in that name, that which had served me just once during my very long existence.

"Yes that's me," I replied.

I signed the docket and observed from all sides the little box which he had given me. There was no forwarding address on the package, nothing which could tell me anything further in the first instance.

Disturbed by this mystery, I went to find Darren, who was sitting in the library doing his accounts. He looked up at me, smiling.

"Yes?"

"I've received a package, or more precisely, Miss Mansard received a package."

Immediately, he stopped smiling. He put down his pen and held out his hand for me to give him the parcel.

"What if it contains a bomb?"

"I can't hear anything suspicious. Open it!"

He combined his actions with his words and suddenly with a swipe of a blade he opened the box. I leaned over the desk to look at the contents: a DVD and a letter. We looked at each other, curious and perplexed. Darren unfolded the letter, which bore the letterhead of "*Immortalis Sangus*" and read it aloud. I listened.

"Miss Mansard,

Did you really believe that killing Professor Moonroe would bring you peace? This man who did so much for you!

He bequeathed us a considerable inheritance and our pursuit of the enzyme will not end with his death. On the contrary, we would now like to honour his memory by pushing forward more than ever.

He left you a little farewell gift we which have enclosed with this letter.

And don't forget that murder is punishable under human law. And you are not above the law.

What you hold in your hands is just a copy of the evidence in our possession, we are not stupid.

See you soon, Miss Connolly,
Immortalis Sangus."

I looked at Darren, I didn't know what to say. They knew who and what I was! They also knew where we lived. All this didn't scare me. We have the means to protect ourselves.

There were only a handful of them, but there were thousands of us.

Darren stood up and we went down to the lounge to play the DVD. At first, the screen was blank; the only thing we could see was the date in the left corner. This had been the day that Lusiana died. This was the day I killed Moonroe. Then, the images started to appear. Unbearable ones. The film had started earlier in the day, at the moment when they had begun to drain Lusiana of her blood. She said nothing. Moonroe asked her lots of questions, but she didn't open her mouth. Her attitude was probably what hastened her death. Moonroe had had enough of waiting for information he would never get, and so decided to hasten the end of my sister. We were watching the images without saying anything. We had much to learn from the terrible reality of humans and their cruelty. After putting all the needles in the body, Moonroe explained that a reverse process would start once she had been drained of blood, and was almost dead. He showed her the cylinders connected to her through the tubes, and he explained that they contained silver which would silence her forever. He asked her one last time to cooperate. When she refused, he set the system going, and her blood began to fill the bags. When the process was reversed and the silver began to poison her, she closed her eyes and died. At that time, we could hear me arriving outside the door. I knew all too well what followed, having lived through it myself. I had no desire to see these images again: I got up, apologised to Darren and left to restore myself again, in the garden. Darren's eyes were firmly fixed on the screen. I was just hoping that he would still love me after viewing the disc. He had only come to help at the end and what he was now seeing was new to him.

Twenty minutes later, he joined me outside. I felt him coming up behind me. He came and pressed himself against my back, and his arms encircled me in silence.

"I love you Lilly."

"I love you more than anything, Darren."

This wasn't over. This was only the beginning.
It was time to awaken our mother.
Because tomorrow...

Find all of my publications on my website:

https://sylvieginestet.wordpress.com/

Join me on Facebook:
https://www.facebook.com/SylvieGinestetAuteur
www.facebook.com/SylvieGinestetTheQuest

Follow me on Twitter:
https://twitter.com/sylvieginestet